HOOKeD

A Fandom Hearts Novella

Cathy Yardley

contents

CHAPTER 1

"Mysterious Pickles Games, how may I help you?" Stacy Fielder said, answering the phone.

"Really, Stacy? Answering phones?" she heard her mother say, her tone irritated. "I thought you were simply filling in for an executive position, not as receptionist. This is why you couldn't meet Martha and me to talk about the foundation fund-raiser on New Year's Eve?"

Stacy winced. Her mother had deliberately avoiding calling her on her cell phone, but she hadn't anticipated a call at work. Whatever she wanted to talk about, she was obviously determined.

"Mom, first of all, I'm the interim office manager, which just happens to include answering the phone," Stacy said, forcing herself to sound reasonable and patient. That she was, in fact, sitting at the reception desk was beside the point. "It's not a huge company. Second, you and Martha do the masquerade ball every year. You've had it all planned since before Thanksgiving, and it's tomorrow night. There isn't anything to talk about, really. So you didn't need me there anyway."

"Yes, but . . ." She sighed. "Well. Maybe you could join us for lunch. We've got some last minute details we'd love you to look over. You know, fresh eyes. Can you make it up to Gianfranco's? Around noon? We should be ready for a break by then."

She sounded breezy, totally casual. But having known her mother all of her life, Stacy was onto her tricks.

"I couldn't possibly. I need to go over to Ain't She Sweet, pick up some things for a, erm, meeting." Actually, she was grabbing cupcakes for her new friend and co-worker Tessa's birthday. She'd worked with Tessa here at MPG for three weeks, but over the past twenty-four hours they'd hung out at Stacy's best friends' bookstore and bonded over a mutual love of *Sherlock, Doctor Who, Mystics*, and all things geeky. Tessa's roommate and fellow coder Adam wanted the cupcakes to be a surprise, which was why Stacy wasn't saying anything aloud about it at the reception desk, where Tessa might overhear. She would've gotten the cupcakes even if she wasn't friends with Tessa, because it was good for company morale.

The fact that it gave her a valid reason to avoid her mother's earnest matchmaking efforts was just a bonus.

"This is important," her mother insisted. "Honestly. Can't you have someone else get it, and stop by instead?"

Stacy's eyes narrowed. "Don't tell me. Martha's got a son, or nephew, or cousin or something who is around my age and just happens to be single."

A slight pause, then her mother huffed. "Stepson. And from what I hear, he's absolutely charming."

"I already fell for charming, thanks." Stacy tightened her jaw.

"Sweetie," her mother pleaded, now sounding sad. "You can't judge all men based on one bad one."

"I know that," Stacy replied, then plowed forward before her mother could interrupt. "No, seriously. Logically, I know that all men aren't con artists like Christian was."

But it wasn't about him, she thought bleakly. It wasn't that she couldn't trust men. It was that she couldn't trust herself—or her own judgment. She hadn't even been attracted to a man, and even those that she thought she might eventually develop an interest in, she'd second-guessed herself.

"You made a bad choice," her mother said, snapping her out of her thoughts. "But you've made good choices before. Remember Lloyd Weathers? He was lovely. Polite. From an impeccable family."

And here it comes, Stacy thought, already pulling out her preemptive ibuprofen and popping out two capsules onto the table.

"Lloyd is still single, you know," her mother said, with obvious, calculated casualness. "And he's still in the area."

"I broke up with Lloyd in high school, Mom," Stacy said.

"He's matured since then, I'm sure. And you wouldn't know unless you—"

"Mom, *please*."

3

Her mother made a *hrumph* sound. "You're young, and it's easy to get misled by some fast-talking, good-looking man. They count on that, in fact."

"I'm twenty-six, not eighteen." Which made the fact that Christian had duped her out of two hundred thousand dollars a little more than a year ago all the more mortifying.

"Trust me. That's still young," her mother said with annoyed affection. "That said, you're not getting any younger. There are plenty of eligible young men that are from good families, families we know—with enough money that you'll know for a fact they're not trying to rob you of yours."

"Mom, I don't want you and Dad setting me up anymore." Stacy was pleased her voice stayed firm. "I'm serious."

"Well, are you at least bringing someone to the masquerade ball?"

At least Stacy could smile at this, feeling some of the tension between her shoulder blades release. "Yes. I'm bringing several somebodies, in fact."

"Several? What do you . . . oh. The girls." Stacy heard the eye-roll in her mother's voice. "Well, I'm sure they'll be . . . memorable."

"We also agreed to do that little promotion for the bookstore."

"It's a benefit fund-raiser, not a yard sale," her mother said primly. "Nothing so tacky as flyers, correct?"

"Don't worry. We'll all be tasteful." Stacy frowned, suddenly unsure what Mallory would end up wearing. "Well, most of us."

"But will you bring a date?" her mother pressed.

Stacy sighed. "I've been on dating sabbatical all year," she said. "That technically includes New Year's Eve."

"A year is a long time, especially at your age."

"Thought you said I was young," Stacy said, then gratefully saw the other line light up as another call came in. "Need to go back to work, Mom."

"We're going to talk about this more," her mother warned.

"And I look forward to it. Love you," she said, then hung up, clicking on the other line. "Mysterious Pickles Games, how may I help you?"

"I was wondering if you could bring me a cup of tea," a low, sexy British voice said.

She blinked, staring at the phone blankly, then looked up when she heard chuckling.

Rodney Charles, one of the coders, was leaning against a nearby wall, talking on his cell phone, staring right at her. In the three weeks that she'd worked here, he was the only one of the guys who hadn't asked her out, it seemed . . . something she appreciated. He winked, shutting off the phone. "Sorry. Seemed like you needed an escape there."

"You have no idea," she said, feeling both grateful and embarrassed.

"Oh, I've an idea, right enough," he said. "Seems like my mum calls weekly to see if I've any plans to procreate and carry on the family name."

"Really?" she said, surveying him. He looked to be in his late twenties, although the twinkle in his eyes made him seem even younger. "Is that a concern? You look like you've got plenty of time."

For a second, a somber look crossed his normally cheerful face. He was striking—deep cobalt blue eyes, black hair, a trimmed beard that only accentuated those turn-quick-and-I'll-cut-you chiseled cheekbones. He was damned good-looking with a wicked grin.

With a serious expression, though, he was downright mesmerizing.

"Yes, well," he said, shaking off the moment with a flippant gesture. "She's concerned that I'm too focused on sowing oats of some wild sort. Which is nonsense. I've told her repeatedly: I can't even keep a houseplant alive, much less oats."

She smirked. "I'm guessing you've sowed plenty."

"Do you, now?" He leaned on the reception desk. "Given it much thought?"

"Not really," she said, quickly and emphatically. "I'm allergic to oats like yours, pal, so eyes front."

"Seems like you're allergic to everyone's oats," he pointed out. "I heard you say something about a dating sabbatical. Sorry, didn't mean to eavesdrop, but you were just out here at the front desk," he added, obviously unrepentant.

6

"I decided to take the year off from men. And women, before you ask."

His eyes widened with amusement. "I wasn't planning to, but thank you for that vivid image."

"Sorry. José hit me with that one." She shook her head, then palmed the ibuprofen and downed them with some water. "Relationships are headaches. I don't need any more headaches."

"True." he said, nodding sagely, then grinned, one of pure deviltry. "Of course, that doesn't discount, ah, oat farming."

"Moratorium on that, too," she said. "Which Steve from marketing could've told you, since he made a similar offer."

"That was more of an observation than an offer, but I suppose it's good to know." His expression turned sincere for a second. "Truly, though—you looked upset, and getting more so. And I sort of specialize in family headaches." He winked. "Keep your chin up."

"Keep calm and carry on, right?" She smiled. "That's so British."

"As I am," he said, tipping an imaginary hat to her. "Right to the marrow, love."

She watched as he waltzed away, heading back to his office down the stairs. She felt a little tingly squirm of admiration.

"Stop that," she scolded herself . . . then decided to sneak one last peek at him as he was walking away. Those blue eyes, that devilish smile, those were intriguing. But let's face it: she hadn't even casually dated in a year. Was it any wonder she wanted to check out the bod, as well? See if it matched that fallen-angel face?

Oh, my.

He wasn't bulky with muscle, but he obviously had a decent physique. And it might be a tad objectifying, but . . . *damn*. That ass in a pair of jeans? She felt her body heat like she'd just stepped in front of the heating vent.

He stopped just before the stairway and looked over his shoulder (*damn, those shoulders too*, she thought, biting her lip). "Let me know if you see anything you like," he called out with a jaunty wink. *Busted*, she thought, and quickly buried herself in filing as she waited for her blush to cool off. There was a reason why she was on a dating moratorium. The absolute last thing she needed was a sexy-as-sin Englishman, who was a player with a capital P, ruining all her carefully built defenses.

CHAPTER 2

An hour later, Rodney was still thinking about his exchange with Stacy as he typed away at code. Just routine programming at this point—he was waiting for the next project to come down the pipeline and almost all publishers were shut down for the holidays, so he was just killing time. His own phone jumped to life beside him. Seeing the number, he smiled.

"Hello, darling," he said. "It's odd, I was just talking to someone about you."

"Don't *darling* me," his mother, the Dowager Duchess of St. Charles, said sharply. "I'm still unhappy you missed Christmas."

"I am sorry about that, but the weather was terrible. Also, we had a late release we needed to go to the wire on," he said.

"You know none of that makes any sense to me." She sighed. "You've been there three years already. Aren't you done having your fun?"

He felt his muscles tense. So it was going to be *this* conversation again. "It's my job, Mother."

"Your job. You realize how utterly horrid that sounds. How *plebian*." He could envision her grimacing. "Bad enough that you try to speak like those low-class friends of yours with that hideous slang—'mate' this and 'love' that and whatnot—but *really* . . ."

"Now, now. Let's not dabble in class warfare," he said, hoping to head her off at the pass. He was also trying not to snicker at hearing "mate" out of his mother's patrician mouth.

"You are Roderick Andrew Murray Fitzclarence, the twelfth Duke of St. Charles, Earl of Loamshire, and one of the British peerage," she said, gaining steam. "Not this little 'Rodney Charles' you keep playing at. You could probably buy that little company twenty times over, and there you are, at their beck and call. At Christmas!" She was quiet for a second. "Your father would be scandalized."

He rubbed his head. Like Jacob Marley, his father was a ghost that usually visited around Christmastime, even though the man had been dead for some twelve years now. "Mother, must we? Haven't we exhausted this avenue of conversation?"

"You are the duke," she repeated. "You're not getting any younger—and Lord knows, neither am I. At what

point will you buckle down and tend to your responsibilities?"

"What responsibilities?" he countered, lowering his
voice and shutting the door. "I keep an eye on the family
investments. I ensure that my sisters are taken care of.
And employment is hardly scandalous. Most of the other
members of the peerage work."

"At *respectable* jobs," she countered. "They don't work
in denim and T-shirts at silly little games!"

"More's the pity, the poor bastards," he said, through
gritted teeth. "These 'silly little games' are my passion. I
love working on them."

"Spoken like a toddler," she said. "Keep being imma-
ture, and you'll never have children of your own."

"My four sisters all have progeny," he shot back. "If
you're feeling remiss in grandmotherly duties, I'm sure a
nice visit will calm your sensibilities."

"You know very well that only you can produce the heir
to the title!"

"I'm twenty-eight," he said, remembering Stacy's observation. "There's plenty of time."

"Anything could happen. You have no idea how much
time you have," she said, her voice solemn, and he knew
she was referring to his father, yet again, who had unex-
pectedly died of a massive heart attack while returning
from the bank.

"I may move back to England," he said, a small effort
at comforting her. "But right now, I'm learning too much,
doing too much, here."

"And still chasing around those women, I imagine." She sniffed. "Not a one suitable to be a wife and the mother of your children, I might add."

He held his breath and mentally counted to ten. "I'm not having this conversation." But it was too late. Memories rushed to the fore, back when he was still at university . . . when paps had followed him as tabloid fodder. When women had thrown themselves at him—or, more to the point, at his title. When he could've had sex with any woman who crossed his path, but didn't, especially after one of those times resulted in a woman throwing a false claim at him and trying to get him to pay her to shut up, even after her claims were proven patently false.

He shuddered. There was a reason he no longer went by his family name.

His mother paused, then sighed softly as they reached the usual impasse. "I suppose it's too much to ask if you're coming home for New Year's?"

He'd considered doing just that, but in his current frame of mind, he realized there was no way. "I can't," he said. "But I will try to be home for a visit the month after or so."

"Very well." She sighed again, a demure, restrained exhalation. "I'm sorry we had words. But this is important."

"I know, Mother. Love to the girls," he said, then rang off, putting the mobile phone down on his desk.

She hadn't understood. He'd mourned his father, although the two of them had never been close. He wasn't necessarily that close to his mother, either, although he felt more affection for her. He knew how much his pres-

ence here pained her. It represented a clear threat to the legacy that she was trying so hard to preserve.

But he wasn't kidding. Games were his life. They'd been a salvation for him at boarding school. It was through mass multi-player games that he'd befriended Fezza. He'd studied computer engineering and programming when most of his mates were studying law or finances. That was how he'd gotten the job here at MPG.

He'd done too much to get this far. He could've been partying in Ibiza or skiing in the Alps, like his rich and reckless cousin Gerard. But even though he was "roughing it," he was still happier here than he'd ever been anywhere else.

There was a light tapping on his door—more like a light kicking. Puzzled, he got up, and opened it.

Stacy was standing there with a tray.

"You called," she said, smirking. She proceeded to put the tray down on his empty desk. "Requesting a cup of tea, remember?'

The tray held a teapot, a teacup and saucer, a strainer, a small pitcher of milk, and a bowl of sugar.

"How do you take it?" she asked, her smile widening.

Stunned, he replied, "Ah, milk and one. Thanks."

She poured the milk into the cup, then deftly poured the tea into it, removing the leaves once they'd served their purpose. She stirred in one spoon of sugar. "Hope it's up to standard," she said. "It's been a while."

He took a sip, and moaned. "Oh, God," he said. "You have no idea how long it's been since I've had a decent cup of tea. This is brilliant."

"Least I could do," she said. "Thanks for this morning."

"No, this is above and beyond," he said, feeling genuinely grateful. "I insist. I must pay back the favor. What can I do?"

"I don't know." Her laugh was soft, the light in her eyes dancing. "What are you good at?"

"Ah, love, the places I could go with a setup like that," he said ruefully, and she rolled her eyes, but her smile broadened. "I have a wide and varied skill set with a very creative range, or so I've been told."

"Jack of all trades, master of none, hmm?" She raised one perfectly arched eyebrow at him, crossing her arms, even as she tried to rein her smile in.

He chuckled. He liked the way she teased back, the way she dressed prim and proper, but had that generous, sensual mouth.

"Rather than ask what I'm good at," he said, leaning toward her and shooting her his best devil-may-care smirk, "perhaps the better question is: what is it you want? What is it you . . . need?"

He was about to wiggle his eyebrows, to show he was joshing her. But her gaze met his, and what had felt like joking about shifted, melting into something else: a sharp, heated awareness that shocked him enough to hold his breath. He noticed that her breathing was shallow. Her hazel eyes dilated, her full lips pursing for the barest of moments. For a split second, hunger crossed her face, strong enough to startle him—and to jump-start a hunger of his own.

"Anything, Stacy," he said, his voice rasping slightly. "Tell me. Whatever you want." She quickly shuttered her expression—something he imagined she was good at by now—and shrugged.

"I'll let you know the next time I need my car washed," she said, her voice bobbling slightly. She cleared her throat. "Enjoy."

With a cheeky—if shaky—grin, she left him with a perfect cup of tea, and a libido that was considerably stirred up.

As he sipped with a fervent sense of comfort, he thought about her. She'd been surprisingly thoughtful, gone out of her way. She obviously hadn't just had this stuff tucked away. It wasn't some loose, cheap quality, paper-bagged tea-dust from the shops. It was something special, a delicious Earl Grey with just the right amount of bergamot and full-bodied black leaves. The water was boiled, not lukewarm, and she'd poured the milk first, like she knew the proper way to do so . . . how Brits took tea.

She was gracious, and grateful, but kept up a wall. Open, but somehow aloof.

She wanted him, but seemed almost scared—more of herself than him.

And wasn't that fascinating?

She was working temporarily as the MPG office manager. Her car and clothes bespoke money, so why the job? What was she doing here?

It was definitely a puzzle.

He grinned.

Luckily enough, puzzles were his absolute favorite kind of game.

CHAPTER 3

The guys were playing pool on the table near the Pit, enjoying draft beers. It was awesome. None of Rodney's old mates from Cambridge could say that their offices were similar to a pub.

"Say, Fezza," he said, pulling his friend aside. "I was wondering. What's the deal with Stacy?"

The mere mention of her name had all the guys looking over at him and he suddenly wished he'd been a bit more discreet. Fezza was shaking his head before he'd finished the sentence, leaning on the pool cue.

"No-go, man," Fezza said. "Seriously. We've all made a run at her. Nobody survives. Even you would crash and burn."

"Nobody said anything about making a run at anyone," he said. "Good God. You make it sound like I was planning on strafing her like a B-52 bomber."

"Every single straight guy here has asked her out," Fezza continued, oblivious. "I asked her out the first day. She was nice, but shot me down in under two minutes."

"I made thirty seconds," José said. "And that was on the first attempt."

"How many attempts have you made?" Rodney asked.

"Not like I keep count." José shrugged, then sighed. "About ten. The last time, she said no before I even started talking. It's how she says hello now."

"Well, that's not stalker-esque or anything," Rodney said, now somewhat appalled on Stacy's behalf. He'd had some audacious and persistent women pursue him when he'd still been hitting the club circuit with Gerard, and he knew how draining it could be. How much worse to be a woman, stuck in a building with that kind of obstinance?

"The delivery guys ask her out, too," Fezza added.

"Seriously. Freezer burn. She's not having it."

"All right," Rodney said. "But I didn't ask about your 'attempts' at her. I'm asking, who is she? What's her story? Why is she even here?"

The question seemed to take them all aback.

"Well, she's the interim office manager," José said, as if he was an idiot. "She's here to . . . you know, order things, make sure repair men get called, set up meetings. Stuff like that."

"You're just messing with me now, right?" Rodney stared at them. "Beyond the fact that she's the office manager and she's shot you all down, do you know anything about this woman?"

The guys all stared at each other for a second, then stared at him as if he'd grown another head.

"She's nice," José finally offered. "Even when she's pissed at me, she stocks the cookies I like in the break room."

"She also recommended a great vet for my dog, Boo Radley," Fezza added. "When I brought Boo by to say thank you, Stacy didn't mind that he got her slacks all muddy, either. Which is pretty cool."

Rodney waited, but that's all they provided. "Some observant lot you are," he muttered.

"Why do you want to know?"

"She doesn't make sense," Rodney said. "Everybody else here makes sense. You guys, the execs. I know about just about everyone in the building . . . except her. I don't like not knowing things."

"You know who I saw her talking to yesterday? Tessa. The chick from audio," Fezza said with a nod. "Stacy asked Tessa if she wanted to go to some book club or something, hang out. So there you go."

"She likes books?" Rodney smiled. He could see that. The thought of her, curled up with a book, drinking tea . . .

"No," Fezza said, with a touch of exasperation. "It means maybe she's gay, dude."

"Ohhh," José said, nodding. "That makes total sense. Man, I feel like an idiot. Although she could've just said so. Felicia in character design is gay, and she's awesome, in a touch-me-and-I'll-kill-you kind of way."

Rodney shook his head. He enjoyed his friends, but sometimes they were so bloody clueless. At least it gave him a lead to follow, though. He decided to head upstairs, toward the cubby where Adam's roommate Tessa did her work, getting audio tracked for the games.

She had her back to him and was furiously scribbling something on a pad of paper. He tapped on the cubicle frame. "Tessa? You have a second?"

"Huh? Oh, sure," she said. She shuffled the papers away, but not before he saw she'd been sketching out levels. Then he remembered: she was planning some kind of video game, with a ludicrous deadline. "Did you change your mind about helping me?"

"Still thinking about it," he demurred. "Actually, I was coming to you with a request."

"Oh?" She turned her chair, facing him, looking puzzled.

He cleared his throat. "I understand you, ah, hung out with Stacy? Book club, or something?"

"Oh." Her stare was withering. "Looking for tips or tricks to help get her to say yes, huh? She shot you down, too?"

"I hadn't asked her, actually," he said, feeling a little offended. "I'm just trying to get some background information on the girl, that's all. I'm curious about her."

"You and every other guy in the building," Tessa said, rolling her eyes. "Not that I blame you, she's really nice, but honestly. If she doesn't want to date, can't you guys just leave her alone?"

"But why doesn't she want to date?" Rodney asked, dropping his voice and ditching all pretense of aloofness. "Do you know?"

Tessa shrugged. "We didn't talk about it. I barely know her. She's nice, but it's not like we're that close."

He waited. Then gave his best, most beseeching puppy eyes.

He was rewarded when she snickered. "Seriously. I just started hanging out with her literally yesterday. I wound up talking to Stacy and Adam yesterday about ordering coffee, and we talked about both liking the show *Mystics*. Next thing I know, she invited me to hang out with her friends at this bookstore."

"And you went?" Adam's roommate was a legendary introvert. "Why?"

"Well, Adam sort of nudged me hard," she admitted. "But once I was there, it was really awesome. I talked with her and her friends a ton—I mean, not just a ton for me. She's really easy to talk to, and her friends are all geeky like me. We talked fandoms, and then I came up with the idea of the game to help them out, and Stacy was really happy with it. They're like her family." She wiggled her eyebrows. "I'll bet it would really impress her if you helped me out with this game, for example."

He filed that idea away. So, her friends were her family? He knew what that was like. Still, he was like a starving man, devouring any crumbs of information he could find. "What are her fandoms?"

"She's a *Mystics* fan," Tessa replied. "She likes comic books, although she's more into Neil Gaiman's *Sandman* and DC than Marvel. She's a big Disney fan, though—loves *Once Upon a Time*."

Rodney nodded, mentally taking notes. So she liked action and adventure, especially when laced with humor. She was cerebral—Neil Gaiman was not for the faint of heart, after all—and perhaps had a bit of a dark side, which might explain the aloofness. But the Disney, now, there was a real clue. She was a romantic, he'd bet. She liked fairy tales. On some level, she believed, and perhaps craved, a happily ever after.

Tessa snapped her fingers, as if remembering something. "Oh! And she really likes *Doctor Who*."

"Excellent," he said, grinning. He would have a hard time getting involved with someone who hated the Doctor.

Wait a second. Who said anything about "involved"?

He shook it off as his brain made another connection. "Wait a tick. You just said they were her friends at the bookstore. Would these be the same bookstore people for whom you're creating the video game?"

Tessa nodded. "Yeah." Then it was her turn to make cartoonishly exaggerated puppy eyes at him. "So, you'll help with the video game?"

"Throw in some fresh-made chocolate biscuits, and I can probably be persuaded," he said around a laugh. Her phone rang, so he waved his thanks as she answered it, and walked toward the reception desk.

He'd asked the secondary sources. Now, it was time to go straight to the subject herself.

He caught her at her desk as she was getting her coat on. "Headed out to lunch?"

"Have to run an errand," she said, grabbing her purse.

"Care for some company?" he offered. "Perhaps I can drive you?"

She smiled. "No offense, but I've seen your car. I'm not even sure it'd make it back to the office."

"Fair enough." He wasn't about to explain that it was Fezza's car, since they usually rode in together. "What's the errand?"

She glanced over her shoulder, her voice dropping to a whisper. "Secret mission."

"Now I'm intrigued," he whispered back. "It wouldn't have anything to do with those bookstore friends of yours, would it?"

Her eyes widened in surprise, then narrowed with suspicion. "Not exactly. How do you know about them?"

"Tessa mentioned them," he said. "She asked for my help in programming a video game, and it has something to do with them. I wondered if you could tell me a bit more about it."

She studied him for a second, then shook her head. "Pretty smooth," she said. It didn't sound like a compliment. "So that's how you're going to weasel your way into my good graces?"

"Stacy," he said, "I want to get to know you. That's all."

"That's all for now," she muttered.

"I'm not going to pretend I'm not attracted to you. You'd be foolish to believe that, in the first place, and you're far from foolish," he said. "But I'd like to get to know you, if you'll let me."

She stared at him, and he could see the tension, the inner war, coiling inside her. Finally, she let out a short exhalation.

"Fine," she said. "I'll talk to you about the bookstore, because I'll bet Tessa could use the help."

"That's fine," he soothed.

"And no comments on my driving."

He grinned, holding the front glass door of the building for her and ignoring her scowl. "Somehow, I will refrain."

"And no . . . funny business," she said as they walked briskly to her car.

"I will be the absolute embodiment of stoicism." He schooled his face into a somber nod. "I'll do my schoolmasters at boarding school proud."

She took a look at him and giggled. Then she sighed. "This would be a lot easier if I didn't like you."

"Now, love," he said, grinning back. "Why in the world would I make it easy?"

Stacy was irritated. Not with Rodney, necessarily. She had a grudging admiration for how neatly he'd maneuvered his way into accompanying her. Her friends were her family, her support network, the people she loved most in the world, so asking about them and Tessa's plan was smart on his part. Beyond that, the guys who had asked her out—both here at MPG, and before, in schools or in her parents' social circles—had rarely asked about her. They were usually too intent on impressing her with stories about themselves.

Rodney didn't really talk about himself, she'd noticed. He was charming and flirtatious. He paid attention.

No, the reason she was irritated was that *it was working*. She found herself charmed.

Damn him.

"So, what is this secret mission?" he asked her as they drove down the freeway.

"We're just grabbing cupcakes for Tessa's birthday party," Stacy replied. She shifted gears and passed a sedan that was moving too slowly.

"Right then," Rodney said, his voice sounding strained. "Not to be 'that guy,' but do we need to go quite this fast to do this? Do the cupcakes self-destruct or something if we don't reach them in time?"

Stacy glanced down at the speedometer—they were inching toward ninety. "No comments on my driving, remember?" she joked, but eased off the gas pedal. "Sorry. I do love driving, and driving fast."

"You do it well," he said, relaxing a little. "Fezza says I drive like an octogenarian."

She smiled at his attempt to put her at ease. "I was, erm, distracted there for a second. Work stuff."

"Interim office manager," Rodney said. "You are doing a stellar job, by the way."

She sent him some side-eye.

"I am being sincere," he said. She also noticed that he was still holding the handle on the door frame, and eased her foot off the gas a bit more with a self-satisfied grin. "Not to say Madge wasn't a decent office manager. I imagine she was, in her way. But you're much more assertive. She'd take care of things after they were problems. You take care of things before they are, and make it look easy."

"I'm surprised you noticed," she said, and meant it. Her parents thought she was some kind of glorified lackey.

"I'm a noticing sort of fellow," he said, and she heard the smile in his voice. "You take the job very personally for someone who is only filling in temporarily, if you don't mind my saying."

"Just because I'm not doing it forever doesn't mean I won't do my absolute best."

"Didn't say you shouldn't. I'm just saying it's rare, more's the pity." He seemed to be staring at her, but she refused to glance over at him, keeping her eyes on the road. "What do you do when you're not doing interim work?"

"This and that."

"Ah. Temp work," he said, that delicious British drawl making even something so mundane sound outrageously sexy. *Damn you, British accents!* "Commitment phobic, then?"

She looked over at him, not surprised to see his blue eyes twinkling, and that sexy-as-sin dimple making an appearance just over his meticulously trimmed beard. "You're awfully good at pushing my buttons, Mr. Charles."

"Ah, I shouldn't," he said, his tone more mischievous than sorry. "But you're fun. And to be honest, I do want to know more about you."

"Why?"

He didn't say anything for a charged moment, and she could sense the tension, delicious and taut, between them. "You really need to ask?"

She sighed. "It's not . . ."

"I get it. No, really, I do," he said, and his tone was surprisingly somber. "You may find this hard to believe, but back home in England, I was fancied a bit of a catch."

She thought of how he'd looked, leaning against that wall, staring at her with that little sexy smile. Yeah, she just bet he was "a bit" of a catch.

"It could get rather ridiculous, after a point," he said, and he actually sounded embarrassed. "Not to say I was fending them off the way you seem to be, but I still understand what it's like to be pursued left and right by people you simply don't connect with. Especially those who don't seem to know or care who you really are."

She let out a breath she hadn't consciously realized she was holding. "That's it. Not that I'm . . . I mean, I don't mean to be conceited. Believe me, in high school and college, if you'd told me that men would be crowding me for dates, I would've laughed in your face."

"So what happened?"

She frowned. "There was . . . I, well . . ."

"Ah." He nodded sagely. "The ex."

She turned, stunned. "How did you know?"

He rolled his eyes. "If your absolutely horrified tone didn't tip me off, love, that aghast look on your face would've been the trick," he replied. "He brought you out of your shell, hmm?"

27

"I had just graduated from college. I wasn't sure what I wanted to do with my life, and I was traveling with my friend Rachel." She smiled, thinking about it. That trip was one of the best memories of her life, and Rachel one of her best friends. Or at least, it was one of her best memories until the truth about Christian came out. "Anyway, he paid attention to me. We had kind of a fling in Italy." She smiled. "Imagine my surprise when I discovered he lived nearby, right here in Snoqualmie, when I came home."

She looked at Rodney in time to see his expression go hard. "Quite the shock."

"See? You saw it coming. My parents saw it coming." She sighed. "I . . . well. I didn't see it. Didn't want to see it."

Thankfully, he didn't say a word.

"Anyway, we were together for a year and a half. Initially, he always took me places, got me gifts, and paid for everything. But he was a struggling artist, and I . . . well, I was a trust-fund kid. I didn't have to work. So I'd find myself doing things for him. Little things, at first. Buying dinners, paying for trips, that kind of thing. Got him a car for his birthday."

"But that wasn't quite enough," Rodney said, and she could hear the restrained anger in his tone.

"No. It wasn't." She frowned. "He started getting interested in real estate. He wasn't at all like the artist I fell in love with—or thought I fell in love with. He said he didn't want to feel unworthy, especially since I had all this money. He started making little comments about how I looked, not in an overt way, but in a way that still made me feel off-balance and insecure. Like, 'I like that you don't care what other people think, wearing worn jeans to a fancy restaurant like this.' And all of a sudden, I *was* conscious of what other people thought, and I felt crappy, like it reflected badly on him. He pointed out I was the daughter of the Fielders: a rich, successful family, prominent in both business and social fronts, between my father's real estate enterprises and my mother's charities. He encouraged me to work more with my mother's charity, the Fielder Foundation, which is dedicated to helping school-aged homelessness in Washington State. I did, and I started dressing the part. After a while, I got a full makeover." She gestured down to her wardrobe. "Before I met him, I'd be wearing a pair of jeans and a hoodie with a hole in the sleeve. So I guess I can thank him for that." Her clothes had become her armor, a firm façade of sophistication and aloofness. Her old clothes made her feel too vulnerable now.

Rodney made a low sound in his throat, like a growl. He didn't seem to agree with her assessment. "Then what?" he asked in a tight voice.

The depth of her embarrassment was brutal. "Finally, he said that he wanted my help to invest in something. Something for the two of us. He hit me with it right after he proposed."

"Bastard," Rodney hissed.

She shot him a glance as they pulled off the freeway toward Issaquah. "Yeah. Initially, my parents liked him, at least when they thought he was a good influence, like getting me to join the charity or change my wardrobe. And I have to say, getting their approval and admiration after all that time was weirdly gratifying. And he was so . . . it's hard to describe. Dominant, in a charming way. I just wanted to make him happy after a while. " She took a deep breath. She didn't need to tell him all of this. She barely told *anyone* about this, since it not only showed her own stupidity, but it dredged up all the old embarrassment and shame and bitterness. But he'd asked, and seemed genuinely interested in her answers. "Then, while we were planning the wedding, he vanished. And then that's when I found out he'd forged my signature, had gotten into my passwords, and he'd cleared out a good chunk of my trust fund and personal bank accounts."

"Ouch."

"My family hired a private investigator, and that's how we confirmed he was a con artist." The pain still seared, even after thirteen months . . . but who was counting? "Not only had he targeted me, he had a girlfriend on the side that he was seeing at the same time, one who helped him set up the whole thing. He'd rolled out his plan when I went to Italy. It was terrible."

"Is he in jail?"

"Yes. We got him," she said, feeling at least a little fierce spurt of pride. "Trapped him, helped the detectives, and they nailed his ass. His skanky girlfriend, as well."

"That still had to hurt."

"More than I care to admit," she said, realizing she'd just told him the ugliest story—one she'd only shared with her girlfriends. She pulled into the parking lot of Ain't She Sweet, a small bakery that made custom cakes. He got out, meeting her in front of the car. "Anyway, since then, I've had plenty of offers, thanks to . . . you know, the makeover and all. And then taking on this job at a game company where men outnumber women easily four to one, I'm in testosterone-ville."

"And your parents aren't helping."

"No. No, they . . . Oh, for fuck's sake," she breathed, turning quickly.

"What?" He quickly glanced around. "What is it? What's the matter?"

Not today. Any other day, but not today. She glanced over her shoulder.

Sure enough, standing in front of the cupcakery was her high school boyfriend, Lloyd Weathers—one who still carried a torch for her, the son of a close friend of the family. He was looking the other way, talking on his cell phone. He was wearing a puffy jacket and a fuzzy hat to ward off the chill.

"I swear to God, today is like the Murphy's Law of dating," she said, gritting her teeth. "This guy is going to ask me out, I guarantee it."

"Not that I doubt it at this point," Rodney gave her an askance look, "but how can you be sure?"

"Because he always does."

Rodney quirked an eyebrow, sizing him up. "Too tired to give him an ass kicking? Or at least a verbal dressing-down?"

"Worse. He doesn't deserve one," she said, feeling her heart sink. "His name is Lloyd, I dated him in high school, and he's actually a nice guy. I just have no chemistry with

31

him, and he seems to think persistence will win the day. With any luck, he won't see—".

"Stacy?" she heard him say. "Stacy Fielder? Is that you?"

"Damn it, damn it, damn it . . . Hi, Lloyd!" She put on her brightest smile.

"I thought that was you." Lloyd was a finance guy of some sort—honestly, she'd never cared enough to remember what exactly he did. Some kind of financial planner, she thought. He had a round face and a pleasant smile, his high school physique turning vaguely doughy thanks to deskwork. He lit up, and threw his arms around her in a hug, not quite stepping back far enough when he released her. "I was just grabbing some stuff at the bakery here. I hear they've got amazing cupcakes, and you know I've got a sweet tooth." His smile was sunny and entirely too sincere. "Funny I should find the sweetest thing here in the parking lot!"

"Oh, you." *Oh, God.* "I'm just picking some things up for a friend's birthday . . ."

"No worries, I won't keep you." He looked like was winding up for the pitch, and her mind raced for some way to head him off. "Your folks are going to have that insane New Year's costume party, right? My parents and I are planning to be there."

No, no, no. "Would you look at the time?" she said lamely, glancing at her wrist before realizing she wasn't wearing a watch. She grabbed her phone hastily. "We're going to be late for the party! Better grab those cupcakes. . . ."

"Why don't we go together?" Lloyd's eyes were bright. "You're single now, I'm single. It just makes sense. What do you say? No point in both of us going stag, right?" He chuckled a little, but his look was intent. Intense, even.

Stacy quailed. "I'm so sorry, Lloyd." Then, abruptly, she frowned.

How does he know I'm single? She certainly hadn't spoken with him. Maybe her mother spoke with his. *Gah.* That sounded like something her mother would do.

"You mean you're not going?" Lloyd pressed.

She briefly thought about lying. Anything to get out of this. But she had to go. She'd promised the girls, and she was determined to promote the bookstore. But he'd be there, and then he'd probably pester her or act like they were there together.

All she could do was either go with him, which would give him false hope . . . or just outright crush him.

She'd had enough for one day.

"Sorry, mate, but she's got a date," Rodney interjected. "With me."

CHAPTER 4

As soon as the words were out of Rodney's mouth, he thought he'd swallowed his own tongue.

Both Stacy and the little bug-eyed fellow were staring at him now. "She's going . . . with you?" Lloyd said. His expression was clearly suspicious.

Stacy, on the other hand, looked like someone had given her a good, hard wallop on the bum.

"Yes," Rodney said, a bit more firmly. "We're going together."

"Right." Stacy suddenly nodded like a bobble head. "We're . . . together."

Lloyd's eyes narrowed. "But your mother said you were single. That you wanted—needed—a date to the party."

Stacy's eyes narrowed, as well. "When, exactly, did she tell you that?"

"Just today," Lloyd said, obviously irritated. Rodney realized that the fellow's "nice guy" act was a bit of a put-on; he knew Stacy would feel guilty and thought he'd be able to maneuver her into saying yes because she had a kind heart. *Not today*, Rodney thought, shooting the shorter man a wolfish grin.

"Let me get this straight," Stacy said, her voice sweet as treacle—something that should've been a warning to poor Lloyd, but the man was far too clueless and petulant to hear it. "You spoke with my mother about asking me out?"

"And she said you hadn't been in a relationship since Christian," Lloyd said, as if complaining about a bill of sale. *Jackass!* "They said you've been single for over a year, and that you . . ."

Suddenly he stopped short, his round face turning red.

"That I what?" Stacy prompted, a bit more venom in her tone.

"We were just talking about the party, that's all," he said, quickly backpedaling, or trying to. "You happened to come up."

"I thought you were working in downtown Seattle these days, Lloyd," she said, moving closer to Rodney and putting her arm around his waist. He didn't mind that one bit, turning his face behind her head to hide his grin. In the process, he got a sniff of her scent—freesia, some hyacinth maybe. Floral, elegant. "Issaquah's about twenty minutes away, and that's without traffic. Are you telling me there aren't any cupcake places in downtown Seattle?"

"I heard really good things about this one," he said weakly.

"My mother called you. She probably wanted you to meet me for lunch. When I changed plans, she told you where I'd be." Stacy's words cut across his protests like a blowtorch. "And you thought you'd just ambush me and ask me out."

"Is it really that bad a thing?" He was trying the "poor me" stance again. "We dated in high school."

"For a few months!" she yelped. "The answer, by the way, is no."

"How long have you been seeing this guy?" Lloyd countered, crossing his arms.

Rodney shook his head. *Stop while you're ahead, you ass.*

Stacy's eyes blazed. "I'm not 'seeing' this guy," she said sharply. "I'm screwing this guy."

Lloyd's mouth dropped open. Rodney choked.

She glared at Lloyd. Then, before Rodney could even brace himself, she laid one right on him, grabbing him by the shoulders and dragging his mouth to hers.

For a second, he smiled against her lips, amused by the ridiculous drama of the moment. They'd have a good laugh about it, he thought, once this little ponce was on his way.

Then he felt the silken lips underneath his mouth, the way they trembled, the way she seemed to melt against him, the force turning to pliancy, the anger turning to uncertainty.

Then all thought of laughter seemed to evaporate in the face of a curious heat.

He kissed her, tilting his head, closing his eyes. Tasting her—the rich, sweet taste of her. Rather than conquering, he softened his stance, anchoring her . . . exploring her mouth with his, a slow dance of lips and tongues.

She let out a soft sigh and it was like she'd wrapped him in a satin net. He couldn't have torn himself away if he tried.

She finally pushed away. When she turned back to Lloyd, he looked disappointed, and more than a little pissed.

Rodney would've chuckled at the pouting man if his body hadn't suddenly shot into overdrive. He'd been intrigued by her personality, the combination of cool aloofness and warm thoughtfulness. As he'd heard the story of her ex, he'd felt both protective and ruefully empathetic: he'd been a socially awkward nerd who had suddenly become a "hot commodity" in a combination of lucky puberty and his inheritance of the title. Now, knowing the feel of her lips against his, her body pressed lightly against his own, he realized there was more than just curiosity and empathy: there was an incandescent chemistry. He suddenly wanted this woman, more than he wanted anything he could ever remember. More than he wanted oxygen.

She still leaned against him, her chin up. "Good-bye, Lloyd," she said, with a note of finality that was only ruined by the breathlessness of her voice. Although in some ways, her breathlessness confirmed that there was no way in hell Lloyd had a chance.

She reacts that way with me, mate. Only me. Now he a good lad, and scurry off.

Rodney cradled her against his chest, nuzzling the top of her head and glaring at Lloyd.

"Fine," Lloyd huffed, then turned on his heel and stomped away.

Stacy waited, then she turned to Rodney, hugging him. "Oh my God," she whispered in his ear. "I'm sorry. That was ridiculous."

"That was fun," he whispered back, his beard brushing along her jawline. He felt her shiver against him, and his first instinct was to get her back into the car, drive some-place private, and finish what they'd started. "Screwing me, are you?"

"This was an aberration. Just for show. We will speak of this to no one," she whispered, but still loosely held him. "*No one*, got it?"

"Mum's the word," he swore.

They stood like that for a moment, pressed together.

Then she gasped, and he guessed that she'd finally felt his hardness between them.

"I'd apologize, love," he said roguishly, "but you did sort of wake him out of a deep sleep. Only natural he'd pop up to see what's going on."

She turned a deep rosy blush, and quickly turned. "I'll . . . um . . . get the cupcakes," she stammered, then glanced down. The blush went deeper. "Why don't you wait in the car?"

"I know. Not one word," he repeated, and, despite the ache, he still found himself laughing as she flipped him off and hurried into the shop.

CHAPTER 5

"Thank you so much, Stacy," Tessa said, giving her a quick, tentative hug. "I can't believe you went to the trouble."

"It was no trouble at all," Stacy assured her. "I'm just glad Adam let me know. It was so sweet of him."

"Yes," Tessa said, her eyes searching out the taller man, who smiled back. Stacy hid her grin. There was definitely something brewing between those two. It made her heart ache, with happiness and just a touch—the slightest touch—of envy.

The birthday celebration was in full force down in the Pit. The cupcakes were mostly eaten now. Guys were popping noise-makers left and right, and they'd decked themselves out in paper hats and used blow-outs as makeshift kazoos. Escaping the festivities, Stacy found herself in her office—or rather, Madge's office, when

Madge wasn't out on leave. It was a tiny, windowless room on the bottom floor. She took a big drink of ice water, hoping the ice would cool down her libido.

She'd kissed Rodney. She still couldn't believe it.

Worse, it had felt *incredible*.

She held the cold glass against her neck, despite the fact that it was maybe twenty degrees outside.

She'd always thought Christian was a good kisser, but Rodney—holy hell. He was some kind of Zen kiss master. The Michelangelo of making out.

Just . . . *wow*.

She shook her head, trying to collect her thoughts. She had bigger issues to deal with right now.

She settled into Madge's empty office, the one place she felt sure she could get a moment's privacy, especially with the celebration going on downstairs. Then she took a deep, fortifying breath, and dialed her mother's number.

"What's this about you having a new boyfriend?" her mother asked without preamble.

Stacy blinked. *That was fast.* Her mother sounded incensed. "I don't have a new boyfriend."

"Oh, really? Then why *did* Lloyd Weathers just call me to tell me you're seeing some bearded man and that you were all over him in public?"

"That's a good question, Mom," Stacy said, her voice staying steady and cold as permafrost. "Why did Lloyd Weathers call you? He's twenty-eight, not ten. So why did he feel it necessary to call my mother to tattle?"

"He's concerned," her mother said, her tone snippy.

"Why?" Stacy shot back, snippy herself. "What does it have to do with him? Or you?"

There was a long, pained pause. "All right. I admit. I handled that poorly."

"You think?"

"Still," her mother pressed, "who is this man?"

"This man," Stacy said sharply, "is a poor co-worker who let me manhandle him to prove a point to Lloyd."

"You kissed some stranger?" Her mother sounded shocked.

"You sent my high school ex-boyfriend to a cupcake shop in Issaquah to ambush me?"

Her mother took a deep breath. "Let's just say mistakes were made all around."

"Agreed." Stacy closed her eyes, involuntarily shivering at the thought of kissing Rodney.

Mistake. Big mistake. *Huge.*

"But you're still going to be at the party, yes?" her mother asked in a quieter voice.

Stacy's stance softened, and she rubbed her forehead. "Of course I'll be there, Mom. Even if it wasn't a family tradition, the girls are counting on me."

"You know, let's just have a different policy," her mother said, her voice smooth and cultured, what Stacy termed her "donations" voice when she worked charity fund-raisers. "You just come to the party by yourself and have a great time. Don't worry about digging up a date. Just have fun with whoever's there. Sound good?"

"Sounds great," Stacy said.

"And do you have your costume taken care of?" her mother asked. "Nothing too risqué?"

"It's a ball gown from one of my favorite TV shows," Stacy said. "Kyla made it. Don't worry, though; it covers all my naughty bits."

Her mother tutted. "It'd better. Love you, sweetie."

"Love you, too, Mom." She hung up, then surveyed the phone.

She really did love her parents. When Christian had stolen from her, she'd thought her investment broker father, who typically crushed people in the business arena only, was going to hunt Christian down himself with a tire iron and a host of harmful intentions. Hell, her mother was ready to shoot him, and she'd never held a gun in her life.

More importantly, they'd been genuinely worried about her.

She'd tried to take their forceful efforts at making her happy in stride as a result. Still . . .

"Just have fun with whoever's there," her mother had said.

That should've just sounded casual. But it wasn't. She didn't just trot out the donations voice for no reason.

It took Stacy all of fifteen minutes to hack into her mother's Dropbox account—password Chin Chin, for her mother's Pomeranian—and look at the guest list for the New Year's party.

Sure enough, there were about twenty-five late additions, all of them young, male, and eligible friends of the family.

She hid her face in her hands. "Oh, God." It was worse than she'd thought.

She was Princess Charming—and they were looking to be her Cinderfella.

The worst part was, she hadn't been attracted to anyone since Christian. Sure, she'd gushed over Cillian Murphy and Tom Hardy, and the guys from Mystics were their own special brand of hot, but real-life guys? Especially the guys that her parents were constantly shoving in her way? They'd left her colder than the bitter December wind.

Except Rodney.

She'd been pissed when she kissed him, incensed at Lloyd's presumption, but that had quickly evaporated in the sheer, nuclear *heat* of pressing her lips to Rodney's. The feel of him, hard and lean and masculine, had made her heart race more than she could remember feeling in years. Perhaps ever. That was a disturbing thought.

Maybe it was a fluke? She shook her head. Maybe she was just going crazy. Or maybe it was just rebellion taking hold.

A little knock on the office door interrupted her thoughts.

"Hey . . . are you okay?"

She glanced over. *Speak of the handsome devil,* she thought. There was Rodney, looking adorable, that magical mouth of his smiling, his eyes looking like sapphires infused with pure, sexy mischief.

"I'm fine. I've just found out I'm being set up on the world's worst speed-dating cycle, but what the hell. It's that kind of day."

He chuckled. "You do seem to find trouble, don't you?"

"No. It's locked on me like a tractor beam." She groaned. "Did you need something?"

She couldn't help but notice that he looked at her mouth for a long moment before he spoke. Her stomach fluttered in return. *Not a fluke*, she thought.

"Not particularly," he finally said, his voice a little husky. "The guys wanted to know if they could have a monthly birthday party with those cupcakes. They went through them like locusts, so I have to assume they were a big hit. They said it would improve morale."

She rolled her eyes. "They also said an open bar would boost productivity," she joked. "But okay. I'll look into it."

"I saved you a cupcake," he said, producing one from behind his back. "It's salted caramel–filled yellow cake with chocolate frosting."

Her eyes widened. "It's my favorite. How did you know?"

Now his eyes sparkled in return. "I didn't," he said, his grin broadening. "It's my favorite, too. I hope you realize what a sacrifice I'm making."

"My hero," she said, biting into the cupcake and closing her eyes. "Oh my God. This is orgasmic."

When she opened her eyes, he was staring at her again, his blue eyes shining incandescently. Then he sighed. "Ah . . . yes. Well, enjoy."

She put the cupcake down, swallowing hard. Her heart was starting to pound. "Rodney . . . wait."

He paused, turning back. "Yes?"

"Could you come in, please? And shut the door?"

His dark eyebrows went up, but he did as requested, leaning against the desk. "Did you want me to sit? Are we having a formal meeting?" he teased gently, but his gaze was quizzical.

She cleared her throat, standing up to face him. Her cheeks felt heated and she wondered if she was blushing. "Um . . . about before. Earlier. At the cupcake place."

His mouth did this rakish half-smirk. "The Kiss That Shall Not Be Discussed? We're discussing it?"

"Yes. That." She swallowed hard, as if she still had cupcake lodged in her throat. It was getting a little hard to breathe, and it felt like the heater had kicked up to inferno degrees. "I don't date the guys here."

"Close as I am to this lot, I don't blame you," he said, surprising her. "They've all but put a target and scoring system up when it comes to asking you out." His face showed his distaste with the idea.

She let out her breath. "There is that," she admitted. "It's uncomfortable, to say the least. Like being a 'new fish' in a prison. They can be nice, but sometimes I get the feeling they see me as a body, or a trophy, rather than a person."

She saw him give her a look of profound, almost rueful empathy. *When would he feel so objectified?* she wondered, staring at him.

He shifted his weight. "Are you wondering how I see you?"

She was about to say no.

"How do you see me?"

She bit her lip. She hadn't meant that. Had she?

His blue eyes smoldered, and there was a flash of pure *want* that struck her all the way down to her toes. "I think you're beautiful," he said, his voice deep like a caress. "That's without question. But I also find you fascinating. You've been burned in a particular way, by a particular man, and the pain's still there. But you kept up the makeover . . . like you're hiding."

She took a half-step away from him, startled. She was surprised he could see her so clearly.

"You're competent and detail oriented, but you're not committed. You love your family enough to tolerate their intrusions into your personal life, but you don't seem to have much of a personal life for them to barge into. You're cool, calm, and collected—and you kiss like you could set a mountain on fire."

She gasped softly.

He sighed. "I'm not going to make a move on you," he said, and she found her stomach knotting with disappointment. "I'm not like the others. I'm not going to make you some sort of challenge. But I'm not going to lie and say I'm not interested, either."

"So where does that leave us?"

"Up to you," he said. "It's always up to you, Stacy."

He started to turn, to reach for the doorknob. And she realized—that wasn't what she wanted at all.

47

She put a hand on his shoulder, and he paused, turning back. "Yes?"

"Do you mind . . ." She bit her lip again, fidgeting.

He faced her fully, only a foot apart from her, looking down at her face expectantly. "Do I mind . . . ?" he repeated.

"Can I kiss you again?" she blurted. "Not under duress this time. Not because I'm trying to prove something. Just . . . to see what happens?"

He didn't move forward, but she sensed that he wanted to. "What do you expect to happen?"

She leaned in a little, inching toward him. "I haven't responded to anyone like you in a long, long time," she murmured. "I don't understand it. I need to . . . I *want* to see . . ."

"If it's a fluke? You want to see if it's repeatable?" His voice sounded both amused and strangled as he choked out a laugh. "Like an experiment of some sort?"

She reached up, putting her hands on his shoulders, and his hands moved to her hips.

"Well," he breathed, dipping his head towards hers. "If it's in the interest of science . . ."

There it was—his humor. He was able to poke gentle fun without making her feel stupid, or the butt of a joke. He made her hot, yes. But he also made her feel safe. Happy.

He helped her feel like *her*self.

She framed his face in her hands, and put her mouth on his, her lips brushing once, twice. Gentle, not the full onslaught that she'd pushed on him in the cupcake parking lot. This was a test. An exploration.

It was firm, yes, and just as drugging as last time. Maybe a bit hungrier. She felt his lips moving over hers, coaxing them open. Felt his tongue trace the delicate inner flesh of her mouth as she sighed.

Then *she* moved.

She grabbed him again—*what is it,* she thought, before all rational thought fled, *that makes me want to be as close to him as possible?*—and dragged him against her. She kissed harder and he stepped up the pace, matching her move for move.

She bit his lower lip. He gripped her hips. Her tongue darted into his mouth. He returned the favor, stroking it with his own.

They flipped, so she was against the desk edge. She moved with him to scoot on top of the bare surface. Her legs parted slightly and he stepped between them. She could feel his hardness brushing against her thigh. It should probably have bothered her, but instead it just stoked the fires inside her.

He tasted like chocolate and caramel, rich and dark and sweet.

She wanted to eat him up.

She pulled away to gasp for air, and he kissed her throat, causing her to bite her lip, trying to prevent a loud moan from escaping. "Oh God," she whispered.

They hadn't locked the door. She was in a borrowed office, ready to grind on this guy. It was completely reckless.

She was losing all sense of reason.

She was losing her judgment. Just like she did with Christian.

She immediately froze, nudging him. With a ragged breath, he pulled away. It took him a long minute to regain his composure, but he still somehow managed.

"Well. Quite." He panted. "So? How was the experiment?"

"We blew up the lab," she said, sounding dazed to her own ears.

"I agree," he said. "Dear God, woman. Your kisses should be labeled a dangerous substance . . . lethally intoxicating."

She grinned, her heart still pounding hard in her chest.

"I know I said I wouldn't," he said, his voice still raspy, "but in light of overwhelming new evidence . . . is the possibility of going out on a date in the realm of possibility?"

She looked down at the floor. Part of her wanted to. Other parts of her wanted to go someplace far more private, and do even more intimate things with parts of him, and the hell with dinner.

But her mind was yelling at her. *Be wary. This is how you fucked up last time.*

"I, ah . . ."

He sighed. "No. That's all right." He stroked her cheek. "When—and if—you're ready."

He opened the door and strode out, closing the door behind him.

She collapsed into Madge's office chair. She'd made the right decision, she congratulated herself.

So why does it feel so shitty to do the right thing?

CHAPTER 6

Stacy had managed to fill up the rest of the day, doing work by rote, barely able to keep her head together. Holiday hangover was bad enough—that week-long corridor between Christmas and New Year's when, essentially, nothing got done. But to add all the other shenanigans to it, worrying about promoting her friends' bookstore at the New Year's party, her parents' ham-handed manipulations, and the Lloyd incident, she was pretty exhausted. All she wanted to do was grab dinner with her best friends, maybe indulge in a glass of wine, soak in the tub, watch some *Once Upon a Time*, and go to sleep.

Of course, that kiss with Rodney—both kisses—have nothing to do with your emotional state.

She grimaced. Naturally, her pesky conscience would pipe in at a time like this.

The kisses had rocked her foundations, and reignited feelings she wasn't quite sure she was ready for. She wasn't ready for Rodney, period.

She walked out to her car after locking up the office.

"You useless . . . bloody . . . *slag*!"

She stiffened. That was distinctly Rodney's voice. Maybe she'd been right not to trust her instincts, after all.

He was pacing around his car, grumbling. "Oh, I'm sorry, sweetheart. Come, now. You know I didn't mean it," he said, speaking directly to the car, his voice much gentler.

"How do you not mean 'useless bloody slag'?" Stacy asked.

He spun around, and immediately blushed, which she had to admit was adorable. "Sorry? Oh, lord. I thought you'd gone." He rubbed his hands in front of his face. "Really. Thought I was alone."

He turned away from her, getting back into the vehicle. She took another step toward her car, then heard the sick sounding *zzzt-zzt-zzzzt* of a car refusing to start. She saw him muttering darkly before putting his head against the wheel.

She sighed. They were the last two cars in the parking lot. All the other guys had bailed. She walked over, tapping on the window.

He opened the door. "Really, I'm fine. I've called a tow company."

"And how long did they say that would take?" She grinned slightly. She'd noticed him driving in with Fezza in the vehicle most days, knowing that they carpooled. "I told you your car was unreliable."

"Actually, my car is wonderfully reliable. This is Fezza's," he said. "I swapped cars with him, as he's on a date tonight that he wants to impress. He correctly assumed that Esmerelda here"—he glared at the lime green car—"would probably not be impressive."

"It's not even running."

"No, that she isn't." He let out a breath, and it billowed into steam in the icy air. "You look tired. Go on home, I'll be fine."

But he was starting to shiver, and despite his leather coat and stiff-upper-lip British stoicism, she noticed his teeth chattered slightly.

Sure, she'd meant to avoid him. It was the prudent thing to do. But leaving a guy to wait, what, forty minutes for a tow truck in the freezing cold? That was just cruel.

"Do you have to be here? For the tow truck, I mean."

He shrugged. "Actually, no. I called Ruby's—they're used to towing this old girl at least twice a month. I think Fezza has a punch card. One more tow, he gets a sandwich."

"I'd wait, but I have to go. I'm meeting some people for dinner," she said. "But . . ."

"Please," he said, before she could ask again. "Don't feel bad. After the gauntlet you've had to run with our lot, I don't blame you for being reticent."

His sincerity, and his understanding, warmed her.

"Well, I did ask you to kiss me," she pointed out.

His responding smile was hot. "Yes. That you did. And I enjoyed it immensely." He paused. "But just because you asked me to kiss you doesn't mean I'm entitled to more than that. It's a lady's prerogative. And I don't want to make you uncomfortable."

She swallowed hard, then looked away when his blue eyes twinkled. "You make me very, very . . . not uncomfortable," she breathed, not wanting him to see just how *not uncomfortable* he made her.

After a beat, she glanced back. He smiled at her. Those damned dimples seemed to mock her.

"Admittedly, you make me mildly uncomfortable," he said, and she laughed. "But it's a burden I'm willing to bear if you are."

She refused to be charmed. At least, she told herself that. "It's just—I was really, really attracted to my ex, as well. And that didn't go over so well."

"I see," he said. Then grinned. "Find me attractive, then?"

His outrageousness surprised a laugh out of her. "Apparently, I'm wildly attracted to con men, thieves, pirates, scoundrels," she listed off. "Bad boys. Han Solo, Snake Plissken, Riddick. Especially if they're dashing, though, like Captain Hook in *Once Upon a Time*."

"Sounds good to me," he said.

She paused, remembering Christian. "And liars. Ones that would mess me up. Still feel flattered?"

Even more surprising, his expression turned serious.

"I'm no saint, sweetheart. And you don't have to trust me," he said. "But you might want to think twice about trusting yourself. One bad decision doesn't mean you're a terrible judge of character. Cut yourself a break."

That would've sounded a lot sager if his teeth hadn't been chattering wildly. "All right, this is ridiculous," she said. "Come on, before you freeze to death."

He looked like he was going to be stubborn for a minute, but finally relented. "Where are we going?"

"Back to my car." She pointed to the BMW behind her. "If you stay out here any longer, you're going to turn blue."

"I've seen you drive, woman," he joked. "I may be better off in the cold."

"In," she ordered.

He paused. "I'm giving you space," he said stubbornly, even as he tucked his hands under his armpits, trying to keep himself warm. "You've got your own right to decide. But I don't want to be teased. I know you want me, and I know I sure as hell want you, and that'll probably be an issue at some point. I'm not going to take your pity . . . and I'll be damned if I pick up another man's tab when I haven't done anything wrong."

She thought about it. He had a point.

Of course, if he *was* a con man, wouldn't he say the same? She bit her lip.

"So what will it be?" he said, his blue eyes boring into her.

She opened the passenger-side door, pointing. "I have seat warmers."

"Bloody hell," he muttered. "You play dirty."

Then he got into the car.

She grinned all the way to her door. This might be foolish, but she had to say—it felt right.

CHAPTER 7

Stacy took him up to Snoqualmie. It was only fifteen minutes away from Issaquah, where they worked, and where he lived. He'd been up this way plenty of times, usually to play video game marathons and crash over at his mate Adam's house, a project manager and one of the first people that Fezza had introduced him to when he'd made it to the States. Still, he hadn't really explored the town; he normally simply drove to Adam's and ate whatever was there. He did know they had fairly decent pizza, but as it was, he thought all pizza was fairly decent.

Considering her car, her family, and the tossers that she'd been fighting off, he suspected they'd go to the ritzy Ridge region of the city—an area that Adam usually dismissed as being too "snooty," a far cry from his own more modest accommodations in what they called "historic downtown." In this case, "historic" being "old."

Instead, she drove to a lively restaurant in the heart of downtown, not too far from Adam's own house. The place was packed. When the door opened, there was a crash of sound. People were watching an American football game on the televisions in the bar area.

"Hi, honey," a waitress said, coming up to them and hugging Stacy. "Your girls are here already."

"Oh, good." Stacy grinned, motioning him forward.

"Your girls?" he asked, jostling through people to catch up with her. It wasn't what he'd expected—not a bunch of sports-bar fans. There were elderly people, laughing and chatting, and families with younger kids. It was anything but posh. Bit more like a pub, he thought, and felt himself inadvertently relax.

"I told you, remember? I was supposed to have dinner?"

"Of course." He knew that—she'd mentioned it, hadn't she? He cursed himself. But he couldn't help but wish it could be simply the two of them. Strangely, it wasn't a hormone-driven fantasy of the two of them getting horizontal, or even the desire to wine-and-dine her at some posh spot, with romance and seduction in mind. He genuinely liked talking with her: her wry sense of humor, her openness, her happiness, especially when she talked about her friends. Even her vulnerability.

Well, that little daydream got shot straight to hell. Instead, he'd be surrounded by her girlfriends. Fantastic.

A woman's girlfriends were her guard, and he got the feeling he'd be grilled about his intentions. If they were any friends worth having, at any rate, and he got the feeling Stacy probably had good friends. Which meant if he hoped to be anything more to her, he'd need to clear this hurdle.

He steeled himself. Auditioning, was he? Well then. Let them see how he performed under pressure.

They approached a table where several women sat, laughing and joking. As soon as they noticed Stacy, they called to her, waving, and she hugged them in turn, some across the table. "Everybody, this is Rodney, one of the guys I work with. His car died, and he's had a rough day, so I thought I'd get him dinner."

"Really?" A girl with short, spiky brown hair surveyed him, her eyebrows hitting her bangs. "Well, well."

"Rodney," Stacy said, with a warm, almost mischievous smile. "These are my best friends, Mallory, Hailey, and Kyla." She glanced around. "Where's Rache?"

"Rachel was just giving last-minute instructions to Cressida, who'll be working the shop tonight while Rachel is out with us," said the girl with retro forties hair and a retro dress—Hailey, he believed—getting up and pulling over another chair. "Not that she has anything to worry about. The shop hasn't had customers after four since before Christmas."

Whatever that meant, it seemed to dampen the mood considerably. "It's a pleasure to meet you all," Rodney said sincerely. He pulled out the chair for Stacy, who looked surprised before she sat down.

"A gentleman," the one with the pixie cut, Mallory, drawled with a sarcastic smirk.

59

"Is that what they look like?" Hailey replied. "I've wondered. I thought the last one was in a zoo somewhere in Boston or something."

Uh, this is going to be fun, he thought, steeling himself for criticism.

"Don't mind them," Kyla, a bubbly, plump, platinum blonde in a UW sweatshirt said with a friendly smile. "So you work with Stacy? What do you do?"

"I'm a coder," he said, then cleared his throat. "Computer programmer. I work on the code for video games."

Kyla smiled encouragingly, while Hailey rolled her eyes. Mallory, on the other hand, leaned forward, suddenly interested. "What kind of games?" she asked.

"Um . . . we do puzzle games," he said. "Escape stuff, brain teasers, some mystery-slash-hidden object, though it isn't my preference."

"Console, or web-based?"

"Web-based." He took a sip of water.

"What have your last five titles been?"

"Ah . . ." He scrolled through his memory. "*Devil's Sanctuary, The Lidless Box, Squander, Escape from Treborn Asylum*, and . . . what was it . . . right. *The Imagisanity*."

"Were they successful?"

"Three were top-five ranked by Gamer World," he said.

"What are your plans for the next five years?" she asked, like a shot.

"You mean professionally?"

"Or overall." She leaned forward. "More to the point, what is your intention toward our friend Stacy?"

Stacy groaned.

"No offense, but do I need to retain counsel for this conversation?" he answered with a small laugh.

"He's just a co-worker," Stacy interrupted, shaking her head at Mallory. "Lay off."

Mallory shrugged, relenting. "Sorry. Habit," she said.

"Mallory's a lawyer," Stacy explained. "She's used to cross-examining."

"You're good at it," he said.

Mallory grinned. "You have no idea."

Before she could take up the gauntlet again, he heard a dusky voice behind him. "Sorry I'm late! I was getting Cressida's dinner order."

He stood up, mindful of his manners, and for a second his mind went blank. The woman had raven hair, full ruby lips, and huge violet eyes.

She was, in a word, stunning.

"Hi, I'm Rachel," she said, holding her hand out. "Sorry. I didn't know we had company."

He quickly took a breath. "I'm Rodney," he said. "I work with Stacy."

He glanced at Stacy—only to see her watching him intently. He got the feeling this was a sort of test, conscious or unconscious, of whether he'd become a slack-jawed idiot in the face of her beautiful friend. Maybe she'd use that as an argument for why they shouldn't move anywhere past their two kisses.

Well, he had news for her: he'd seen more than his share of stunning women in his time. But he'd yet to react to one the way he reacted to Stacy, in her tailored khakis and no-nonsense ponytail. Her humor, wit, and warmth were the hooks. And yes, he was absolutely hooked.

"Rachel, of the European vacation?" he said, pleased to see the surprised expressions on all of the women's faces.

"That's the one," Stacy admitted.

He shook Rachel's hand. "Stacy invited me to dinner," he said, meeting her eyes. "My car broke down. She's been my hero this evening."

Stacy flushed. "Really. Not a big deal."

He sat down next to her. Rachel, he noticed, was studying him quizzically.

"Oh! There's the woman who is doing the promotional flyers and swag for the bookstore. I need to talk to her," Stacy said, putting a hand on his arm absently and nodding. He felt the warmth of her fingertips, and smiled. "She's going over to the bar . . . Would you excuse me? I wanted to ask her about New Year's, and the goody bags we were going to make."

"Goody bags?" Rachel said, getting up and following her. "Wait, I thought we were just doing flyers . . ."

The two women disappeared into the throng, leaving him surrounded by the other three.

"So, you're hitting on Stacy," Mallory said, without preamble.

"No," he said. "I am considering wooing her, however. There's a difference."

Hailey smirked, taking a draw from her soda's red straw. "There are some things you need to know about Stacy."

"I know that her last boyfriend screwed her over," he said, deciding to play some defense. "I know he stole from her. I know that he broke her heart."

He looked at all of them in turn.

"And last of all, I know that I'm not like him," he said firmly. "And I know that, since then, every rich ponce in Seattle, and every son or grandson or near acquaintance of her parents seems to have been added to her dance card. I'm not like that, either."

"What? You're not eligible, or you're not rich?" Mallory asked.

He sighed. Two of the things that Britain had thought were important about him. The only two things, really. He made a face. It was yet another reason he loved America . . . and why he kept his title and his wealth on the quiet.

Of course, it's more than simply keeping hush about it, isn't it? Mightn't Stacy take it as a lie of omission?

He pushed the thought aside, focusing on Mallory's question and how to tack around it without revealing his secret. "I'm single," he said. "And I make a decent living at MPG. But if you're worried about me stacking up somehow, or being worthy . . ." His chin went up. "That's Stacy's call, and hers alone. Quite frankly, I don't need to prove myself to anyone else."

They stared at him. "Good answer," Hailey said grudgingly.

"Anything else you'd like to know?" he pressed. "Did I miss anything?"

"Just one thing that you need to know," Mallory said. "She's one of our best friends in the world."

63

"She accepts us the way we are, and given our . . . histories, that hasn't always been easy," Hailey added.

"Bottom line: if you hurt her, we will fuck you up beyond recognition." Mallory smiled, a vicious smile. "Gladly."

"We never got our hands on Christian," Hailey said. "I still regret that."

"And I still say we can rectify that," Mallory retorted.

"He's in *jail*, Mal," Hailey said, rolling her eyes.

"What's your point?"

"Aren't you a *barrister*?" he couldn't help but ask. "An officer of the law?"

Mallory's grin was evil. "Private practice now," she said. "And it means I'll know how to not get caught."

He studied all of them. Kyla, the only reasonable one among them it seemed, was happily munching on some appetizers. "Well, at least I'm safe with you, then?"

She smiled brightly. "I'm a mechanic," she said.

"Oh?" He blinked, wondering what she was getting at. Was she trying to see if he was sexist? "That's a good field. I should bring my friend's car 'round."

"If you hurt my friend," she continued, her smile still brilliant as sunshine, "I've got an acetylene torch, a hydraulic press, and a guy at a car wrecking yard with a crusher who owes me a favor."

Rodney actually skidded his chair back an inch before he could stop himself.

"It's funny, she smiles like sunshine and she seems like Pollyanna, but it's all a front," Mallory said with a smirk. "She's really the one not to piss off."

Kyla clinked glasses with her.

Rachel and Stacy chose that moment to return to the table. "Did I miss anything?" Stacy asked, taking the seat beside Rodney again.

"Nope," he said. "Just getting to know your friends."

"Oh?" Stacy looked at them suspiciously. They all returned the look with angelic expressions of their own.

"They were warning me off a bit," he admitted.

Stacy huffed. "Oh, come on, guys . . ."

"They're right to," he said. "They're good friends. They just want to protect you."

Stacy stared at him, her misty hazel eyes surprised.

"But I'm not a man who scares easily," he added, looking at Stacy's friends with equal determination. "Besides, the best things are worth taking some risk for."

He was gratified to see grudging respect in their responding gazes. He opened the menu, glad to have thrown them off stride. "So tell me . . . what's good to eat around here?"

CHAPTER 8

A little while later, Stacy pulled up in front of Rodney's apartment complex. "Well, here you are, back in one piece," she said. "No thanks to my friends. I hope they didn't threaten you too much."

"There may have been mention of torture, dismemberment, and ease of both body disposal and police evasion," he said.

Stacy shut the car off, laughing nervously. "They can get sort of carried away."

"They're your friends," he said with a smile. "You're lucky to have them. I would've given my right arm to have friends like them—before I met Fezza, anyway."

"How did you meet him?"

He laughed, rubbing the back of his neck. "Promise you won't think me an utter nerd?"

She quirked an eyebrow.

"Well, no hope of that, honestly," he admitted. "I was playing *World of Warcraft* online in London and met Fezza on a quest. We just hit it off."

"He helped you?"

"God, no. He killed me and stole all my gear," he said, surprising her, laughter bubbling to the surface. "Later on, I told him off and he felt a bit sorry, so he offered to let me join him on a mission in order to gain new, better gear, since apparently mine was crap. We wound up playing a lot, and then comparing other games, and emailing."

"While he was here, and you were in England?"

"Well, he was still in San Jose with his family, but yes," Rodney said. "We always kept in touch. I studied computer engineering and programming, and a lot of higher division maths . . . and then Mysterious Pickles started up, and Fezza got the job. He thought of me, put in a good word. And here I am."

Here he was. She felt a sugary warmth in the pit of her stomach. Here *they* were.

"Do you ever miss home?" she asked, knowing she was drawing out the conversation. Wanting more time alone with him.

"Now and then," he said, shrugging. "But really, I never quite felt like I fit in there. I fit here."

"Do you have family?"

"Three sisters, four nephews, and a darling little niece," he said, and his smile was warm.

"What about your parents?"

"My father died, twelve years back," he said. "I still have my mother, though."

"Oh, I'm so sorry."

He shrugged. The British stoicism, she thought. Stiff upper lip, and all that.

"Were you close?"

Now she saw a brief flash of pain. "Not really. It isn't really our family's way."

She sighed. "You must think my parents are lunatics," she said.

"I think my mother would probably drink tea the same way as your mother," he said. "Which reminds me: how did you know how to make tea properly?"

She laughed. "Like British tea is the only proper tea," she teased, and chuckled when he rolled his eyes and grinned back at her. "I spent a year abroad, in Sussex. Tea was one thing I really loved."

"You're a natural," he said. "And thoughtful."

She started to shiver, and reluctantly sighed. "Well, it's getting late," she said, "and cold . . ."

He leaned toward her, slowly, and she couldn't help it. She held her breath, all thoughts of cold fleeing in the presence of his utter hotness.

"I told your friends I was considering wooing you."

She blinked. Momentarily, her body went hay-wire—*yes, please! Woo away!*—while her mind started immediately panicking. *Wooing* sounded both archaic and disturbingly serious. "You're what, now?"

"At first, I was simply intrigued by your inherent contradictions: the coolness, yet the sweet warmth beneath it. Your manner. I wanted to puzzle you out. But the more I know about you, the more I want to know, and it's more than simply physical." It sounded like it might be a pickup line, and she braced herself, but the stunned bemusement in his expression made it seem like he'd surprised himself, either by the emotion or the fact that he was sharing it. His cobalt blue eyes were black in the darkness of the car, staring at her intently. "I wanted them to know where I stood. Whatever they planned on threatening me with, whatever they eventually did . . . I don't care. They could have a gun to my head, I still wouldn't care. I want to go further with you."

"Pretty brave words." Her voice shook a little, and her body trembled in a way that had nothing to do with the cold.

"Words are easy. You, of all people, would know that," he said. His voice was low, that accent like mink across her senses. "But you're the only one whose opinion I care about. So I'm putting it to you, plain as I know how: will you go out with me?"

"Go out?" That sounded so juvenile. That voice, that tone . . . it seemed designed for sexy, delicious whispers, seductive invitations.

"Will you let me win you over?"

"I'm not a prize," she said quickly.

"I am," he teased with a rueful note, but she didn't answer with a smile. "If you don't want me, I'll walk away. I'll leave you alone, treat you like a perfect gentleman. All women have the right, the choice. I'll always respect that."

"I . . ." She swallowed. "I shouldn't want you. I barely know you."

"I'm more than willing to let you get to know me," he said, although a faint flicker of something crossed his expression, causing her suspicion to kick up a notch. "Because I think that you trust me more than you realize, but you don't trust your instincts."

It was something Christian used to say, toward the end. *Babe, don't you trust me?* She didn't really know Rodney, and even if she was drawn to him like an electromagnet, she didn't know what he was really like.

She sighed, wondering how she could explain this to him. "Have you ever screwed up so incredibly that you wanted to just die?"

"No," he said. "I'll be honest, I haven't. I've screwed up plenty, but not to that point."

"Thanks, actually," she said. "A lot of guys would've lied, or just tried to switch the conversation to talking about their experiences, or tell me I shouldn't feel that way. And obviously, I've been lied to." She gritted her teeth. "I don't ever want to go through that again."

Another flicker across his handsome face—a look in his eyes. Like . . . guilt? Remorse? Determination?

Her Spidey senses were tingling.

Was he hiding something?

"You feel the way you feel," he said finally, his voice soothing. His expression seemed sincere. Was he just a great actor? It sounded like he cared—like he respected her. Her heart really wanted to believe that. *Damned heart.* "Again, I respect that."

"You confuse me," she whispered.

"As you do me," he countered. "What do I need to do for you?"

Convince me. Make me believe you.

She didn't even know she was leaning toward him until she was almost there, to his lips. Her body had outflanked her brain, and was going for what it wanted regardless of her concerns.

She just wanted a taste, she thought. She wouldn't forgive herself if she just let him get out of the car, told him no, let him walk away, treating her like a polite stranger. Her whole body, her heart, rebelled against that with a surprising fire.

He tugged at her, weaving his fingers into her hair, holding her against him. Their tongues tangled. She wanted him so badly that she ached with it.

She pulled away.

"I'll take it that means you're open to the possibility of being wooed," he said, out of breath.

"That's a maybe," she said. "I can't trust myself, but I swear, you are like heroin. Totally addicting—probably dangerous. Definitely foolish."

"Excuse *you*."

She laughed. "The attraction. Not that *you're* foolish."

And that was the other thing. He made her laugh. Christian charmed her, he wooed her . . . but he hadn't made her laugh. Hadn't made her comfortable. If anything, he'd made her feel inadequate, even with his charm.

"I want you," Rodney said. "I haven't had an attraction like this, either. I've been interested in you. Good lord, seems like everyone has been . . ."

"Excuse you," she tossed back.

". . . but it's more than that," he said. "Damned if I know, but you kissed me, and it's like my brains poured out of my head. I thought you were interesting, funny, personable. But now . . ."

His eyes blazed.

"Now, I feel like I'd face a dragon to get you into my bed."

She gasped, feeling a zing of electricity at the thought of being in his bed. Or hers. *Or, hell, up against wall . . .* "That's straightforward."

"No sense in lying about it," he said, his cobalt eyes boring in on her with intensity. "You feel it, too, don't you?"

She swallowed. There was no point in lying, but it wasn't really a good enough argument, either. "Is that all there is to it, then? Just this . . . chemistry?"

She paused. Actually, if it was just chemistry, that could be the answer to all her concerns. Nothing emotional—nothing endangering. Just flash and heat, bodies pressed together. A few orgasms might even clear her head—and she had the feeling she'd have several with him, maybe all in one session. Her eyes roamed over his body, and her body started tingling in anticipation.

Just a one-night stand, she thought with a smile. Something quick, purely physical.

Something safe.

"No," he said. "Whatever's between us, it's not going to be some one-night stand."

She blinked as her fantasy fizzled away. "What, you read minds now, too?" she grumped.

His wicked grin was lightning fast. "Don't think I haven't considered it," he said. "Just inviting you up, then showing you just how much I want you. Kissing and nibbling and licking all that porcelain skin of yours. Stripping you out of the layers of your silk blouse and wool trousers, seeing what you've got underneath. Lace? Cotton? Either way, I'd coax it off you. Then I'd love every inch of you, teasing you until you were as hot as I feel."

"Oh, my," she breathed. Her skin felt like it was alight.

"Then I'd taste and stroke and bite," he said, his voice growing rougher and more heated, "until you were begging me to enter you. And I would—slow, and then harder, and then bury myself in you until you came screaming my name."

He let out a shuddering breath. She wanted to fan herself. The car suddenly felt about a million degrees.

"And that'd be fantastic, wouldn't it? You could keep yourself safe. No vulnerability. No emotional attachment. Just work you over, make you scream with pleasure, and be done with it."

She shuddered. "Okay. Sign me up."

"It's not that easy," he said. "It won't be. I'm not going to simply be used, and I'm not going to let you cheapen yourself, or what we might have, because you're still hanging on to the past. I'm not going to let you just use me and then walk away because you're not willing to give me the slightest chance that this is more than sex. It's cowardly. You're better than that."

She glared at him. "Well, maybe one of the fifty or so eligible bachelors that are going to be crowding tomorrow night's party will have lower standards," she shot back.

He leaned in, dangerous. Her body, traitorous to the last, thrilled a little bit.

"You aren't going to throw yourself at one of those bloody fools," he growled.

"Why? You won't allow it?"

His eyes flashed . . . then he closed them, taking several deep breaths. "No. Because the woman I . . . know," he said, after a pause, "wouldn't sleep with an ass just to spite me."

She smiled weakly, knowing he was right. "You've got a high opinion of yourself," she teased.

"No. I've a high opinion of you."

She was still for a second. She'd always been afraid of heights, but she imagined this must be what people who bungee jumped felt like, so high off the ground, looking at a huge drop, with the barest string keeping them from total destruction.

"Would you like to come with me?" she asked quietly. "To my family's New Year's party?"

His answering smile was full of tenderness—and pride. Her heart beat double-time.

"I would be honored," he said, leaning forward and kissing her.

Before she could get too distracted—because his kisses were mind-blowing—she pulled away. "It's a masquerade party," she warned him.

"I've never been one of the cosplay types," he said, leaning in and kissing her throat, which coaxed a low groan. "But I can manage. What will you be dressing as?"

"Emma Swan, from *Once Upon a Time*," she said, leaning against his heated lips. "There's this episode where she's wearing a red ball gown at this . . . oh, God, you're good at that."

He chuckled against her collarbone, pulling away. "There's more where that came from, but not for tonight," he said with obvious reluctance. "As to the costume, don't worry, I'll figure out a suitable accompaniment."

"I'll be helping promote my friends' bookstore," she babbled, feeling bereft as he opened the door. "Why don't you meet me there? I'll text you the address."

"All right." He winked at her. "Don't worry, love. It's a party. You'll dance, drink a bit, have a good time. I'll chase off those wankers your parents shove at you. And then afterward . . ."

There was a lot of promise in that word. *Afterward*.

She felt her stomach flip nervously. "Afterward . . . we'll see how it goes."

But she knew exactly where it was going to lead. She just hoped that history wasn't repeating itself.

CHAPTER 9

It was New Year's Eve, and he was *very* late, which he detested. The long line of cars leading up to Fielder House didn't help his temper or his nerves any. The fact that it was close to midnight and someone else might kiss Stacy made him downright homicidal.

He'd probably gotten too hung up on matching Stacy's outfit, but she'd made the point of telling him her costume in great detail: Emma Swan, red ball gown, *Once Upon a Time*. It obviously meant a lot to her. Tessa had mentioned that Stacy was a big fan of the show, and of Disney in general. He'd immediately googled the scene Stacy had referred to, chuckling as the modern character Emma had passed herself off as "Princess Leia" and her date as "Prince Charles." He remembered Stacy saying that she was wildly attracted to pirates and scoundrels like Captain Hook. As a result, he'd spent the past twenty-odd hours tracking down the closest approximation to the costume Hook was wearing in that scene, which led him to several flaky Craigslist ads, a number of costume shops (several of which were closed), and some of José Yao's cosplay friends. In the end, he'd finally grabbed the final pièce de résistance—a tawny gold–colored eighteenth century–styled jacket, which he'd purchased at an outrageous price from someone in Bellingham, a two-hour drive away. He'd transformed himself into the notorious "dashing" Captain Hook.

Now, he had to claim his Swan—or more to the point, his Stacy.

After cursing under his breath and inching his way through the queue of cars, Rodney handed his keys to the valet. Fielder House was a mansion. Not like the mansions he'd grown up in and around, though. Comparatively, it looked a bit rustic, all large logs and Pacific Northwest Arts and Crafts sensibilities that he found quite beautiful in its way. That said, it wasn't his family's seat, the great house in Surrey. Not by a long shot. But then, this was America. Few things came close to an eighteenth-century English castle.

He told the security detail his name at the door, and then entered. The party was in full swing, and he hated the idea that she'd been left to fend for herself for hours, knowing that her family had specifically drafted men to pay court to Stacy and get her into a new, "acceptable" relationship. The men in the crowd seemed to outnumber the women two to one, at least. They'd spared no expense on costumes, either, he noted, and was gratified that his costume accounted itself well. He thought he saw the pasty and irritating Lloyd in attendance, dressed as Han Solo, complete with medal from the end of *Star Wars: A New Hope*. Stacy did like Han Solo, but the rakish element, not the cleaned-up, bemedaled one. *What a knob*, Rodney thought with a derisive shake of the head. At least the toady ex was nowhere near Stacy.

After twenty minutes of searching, Rodney finally caught a glimpse of Stacy talking to Tessa, who was dressed in a white lab coat with a long scarf. He grinned, recognizing Tessa's costume immediately as Molly Hooper from the BBC's *Sherlock* series. Then he got a good look at Stacy, and all thoughts ceased.

She was wearing the red ball gown, as he'd suspected, but the thought hadn't done the vision justice. Her dress was a bright bloodred, making her pale skin look luminous under the warm lighting. Her blond hair was up, trailing a few tendrils that framed her face and curled against her throat. She was searching the crowd, as well.

Looking for me, I hope.

Tessa stepped away, looking at her phone. He sneaked around, creeping up behind Stacy and wrapping an arm around her waist, pressing his cheek against her hair. She stiffened.

He whispered in her ear. "Emma Swan, I presume?"

He felt her relax, melting against him. She shot a quick smile over her shoulder, brushing her back against his front in a tantalizing manner as she turned to face him. "You are very late, Captain Hook," she said, her gaze roaming over him. "But the wait was worth it. That's amazing! How in the world did you get a costume that perfect?"

"What, this old thing?" he said with a cheeky grin, and was gratified when she laughed. "I figured any woman as stunning as you deserved a date that lived up to your expectations. I'll also add that you far surpass mine." He returned her once-over. "That dress is amazing."

"It's a little tight," she said, with a slight blush. "I'm not used to wearing something quite this elaborate, either."

"'Well, you may not be able to move,'" he quoted to her, "'but you cut quite the figure in that dress.'"

Her whole expression glowed. "*Once Upon a Time*. From the scene with these costumes. You really did your homework."

"Damned right I did my homework," he said, causing her to laugh again. "I'm starting a relationship with you, Stacy. I'm not half-assing this. I am all in."

Her eyes widened. Then the crowd around them started chanting.

"Ten! Nine! Eight!"

"It's almost midnight," she said, her voice almost drowned out by the din of the crowd. She leaned closer to him, and he strained to hear her.

"Seven! Six! Five!"

"So it is," he replied, leaning closer to her, holding her waist. Her hands smoothed up his coat, one resting on his shoulder, the other curling around the nape of his neck. He pulled her flush against him.

"Four! Three! Two! One!"

Amidst a flurry of shouted "Happy New Year!" he leaned down and kissed her.

She swayed into him, and he held her tight, one hand on the small of her back, the other firmly in the center of it. She tasted like champagne and sweetness. She melted in his arms, and it was all he could do to keep a rein on his more ravenous impulses.

He wanted her, that much was obvious. But not just for tonight. He knew that. It had been years since he'd let himself be more than simply physically attracted. After being a "coveted bachelor" and a sort of trophy prize in England, he'd simply put off dating and relationships, keeping things casual.

This was the start of a new year, and a new phase in his life. A new approach to relationships.

You've got to tell her the truth. If there was going to be more to them than just the flash of the physical, he had to come clean about his real identity. He didn't regret changing his name to distance himself from his problematic past, but he hadn't expected to meet someone like Stacy, or to experience the physical and emotional attraction he now felt. And he certainly hadn't anticipated her past betrayals—or how his deception, unintentional or not, might hurt her.

They broke off the kiss, breathless, resting their foreheads against each other. He saw her smile. "You were worth waiting for," she said, her voice warm.

"So were you," he said.

I'll tell her. Soon. Tomorrow at the absolute latest. But tonight—tonight is for her.

They spent the next hour enjoying the party together. It was an unusual "date," to say the least, but he made sure that she enjoyed herself. They danced, something he hadn't done in years. He particularly enjoyed the ballads, since it gave him the opportunity to both hold her close and talk with her, exchanging whispers in each other's ears to be heard over the music. He spent a bit of time hanging out with her and her friends, hearing about the bookshop and their efforts. After a while, Stacy sneaked him out of the ballroom and showed him around the house, giving him a full tour.

"This is your childhood bedroom?" he said with smirk. "It's like something for a fairy princess."

She groaned, hiding her face. "My mother's idea. Or rather, her decorator's. I prefer more Arts and Crafts or Shaker styled, but Mom liked something a bit more . . ."

"Baroque?" he asked, tracing his fingertips over the elaborate carvings in the four-poster bed with its ornate canopy. "This looks like something out of Buckingham Palace."

"Don't I know," she said with a giggle. "What was your bedroom like?"

"The one at my parents' home?" he answered, looking over the contents of her bookcase. She had a respectable amount of sci-fi: Heinlein, Butler, Le Guin, Asimov. He'd have to discuss which favorites they had in common sometime. "Also a decorator, but much simpler. My father believed in spartan decoration for boys especially."

"Traditional?"

"That's one way of putting it," he said, thinking of his father. "Distant, more like. He meant well, but he had high expectations for how a young man in his family ought behave. It could be . . ." *Painful? Exhausting?* "Tiresome," he finished.

Dealing with his family and their expectations, the burden of their wealth and title and its subsequent attention, was something he'd gladly put behind him. They were alone. He ought to tell her now, he supposed. But he wanted her to just get to know him, if only for a few hours more.

She seemed to understand his swirling emotions, giving him a half hug and a gentle smile.

He cleared his throat and shook off the heavy emotion. "When I went off to school, my room truly became *my* room, though," he continued. "I had posters of *Assassin's Creed* and *Mass Effect* and *Halo*. I was game geek extraordinaire for a while there."

"No shame in that," she said.

He glanced at the four-poster bed, wiggling his eyebrows. "And did you get up to any shenanigans in that bed, missy?"

"I told you: I was a late bloomer," she said with a snicker. "I didn't get up to anything in that bed."

"Missed opportunity," he noted. His body clamored momentarily, but he shut himself down. This was her chance to get to know him—not for him to get pervy and take her on her childhood bed. "Come on, let's get back to dancing."

Another half hour, and he was feeling tired but happy, especially when he saw the smile on her face. "This is a gorgeous place," he said.

"It's way too big for just my parents and me, but my father likes things that are showy," she admitted. "He's got a big personality. You get used to it."

"I don't know that I ever got used to my father's," he said without thinking, then saw her surprised expression. "About my family. I should—"

"Stacy!" A woman's voice called out through the carousing crowd. "Stacy! Over here! We've been looking for you!"

Stacy groaned. Rodney pulled back enough to see an attractive middle-aged woman with Stacy's gold hair waving at them from a nearby dais. She was wearing an elaborate sky blue gown with a crown of what looked like crystal snowflakes, as well as carrying a snowflake wand.

"Is that your mother?" he asked.

Stacy nodded. "I've been avoiding her all night. I guess I might as well get this over with."

"Is she supposed to be that girl from that *Frozen* movie? Elsa?" he murmured in Stacy's ear as they maneuvered through the crowd. She let out a low, strangled chuckle.

"Nope. Glinda the good witch . . . from the Broadway show, not the movie," she explained. As if that cleared up the answer for him somehow, he thought, swallowing an amused chuckle. "My dad should be dressed up as Sky Masterson from *Guys and Dolls*. Here I am, Mom," she finished as they stepped up to where the woman stood.

He would've guessed they were related: her mother had Stacy's hazel eyes and high cheekbones. The stoic-looking man next to her was dressed in a pinstripe suit and fedora. He had salt-and-pepper hair and a strong jaw. He towered over the relatively petite Glinda. Stacy had gotten her height from her father. His eyes were the coldest brown Rodney had ever seen as the older man sized him up.

"Stacy, I wanted to introduce you to Peter. You know, Edward's son? Your father's lawyer," her mother said, linking her arm in Stacy's and starting to tug her away. "We've been looking all over for you. There are several people who are eager to meet you, and it's getting late."

"Mother, if we're making introductions, let me introduce you to my date," Stacy said, stopping her mother before she could drag her off. She turned, gesturing to him, and Rodney felt his back straighten as he held out a hand. "Mom, Dad, this is Rodney Charles. I work with him at MPG. Rodney, these are my parents, Helen and Terrence Fielder."

"Pleased to meet you," he said smoothly.

They stared at him for a long second as he shook their respective hands. Gaped at him, perhaps, was the better phrase.

"I'm sorry. Rodney . . . Charles?" Her father's stare was piercing. "I don't believe Stacy's ever mentioned you." He glared at her for a second, as if chastising this state of events.

"We've only recently started dating," Rodney said quickly. "We went out to dinner just once, and she was kind enough to invite me here. You have a lovely home."

Could he sound like more of a kiss-up? He winced. It had been a long time since he'd even thought of impressing someone's parents. He felt like a teenager, for God's sake.

"So it's nothing serious, then?" her mother asked, her hazel eyes seemingly guileless. "Just . . . friends?"

"*Mother.*" Stacy groaned again, covering her face with her hand.

Rodney put his arm around her waist. "More than friends," he said firmly.

Both parents' eyebrows went up in surprise, and in the father's case, disapproval.

"Oh! Well, that's . . . nice." Stacy's mother's voice bobbled. "So . . . you're a computer programmer, then? Working on video games?"

"Yes, I am."

"And what about your family?" her father said. "From around here? You sound British."

"My family is back in England, yes," Rodney said, feeling uncomfortable. He hadn't really thought through meeting her parents, although he should have. If he came clean now, they'd probably be duly impressed, but he was afraid it would be a terrible shock to Stacy. He wanted to tell Stacy the truth, but not like this—not as a surprise, in front of her parents. It was something he wanted to discuss with her in private.

Dammit. He'd been so intent on impressing Stacy he'd never even considered the fact that her parents would want to meet him, or that Stacy would want him to meet them. Of course, it was their house, and they were trying to get her married off to any one of the eligible bachelors here. Naturally they'd be an obstacle he should have foreseen!

"What do your parents do, Rodney?" her mother pressed.

He stiffened. "My mother is . . . retired," he said, figuring that was close enough to the truth. "My father passed away some years ago."

"Oh!" Helen blushed. "I'm so sorry."

"How long have you two known each other?" her father asked before he could respond to Helen's condolences. "Again, this is the first I'm hearing of you."

"Stacy and I know each other from work, since she started there," Rodney said. "It's been a few weeks. We've only gotten to know each other better recently."

"Is that so?" There was distinct challenge in her father's voice. "Your idea, or hers?"

"Dad . . ." Stacy's voice held a note of challenge of her own. "Please."

"I'd say it was a mutual decision," Rodney said, with a sharp note of his own. "Seeing as Stacy is a grown woman and capable of making up her own mind about the company she keeps."

That was probably rude. He looked to see if Stacy was offended. Instead, he saw a glow of admiration in her eyes.

"My daughter hasn't shown the best judgment in that arena in the past," her father pressed, and Rodney stared at him. *You did not just say that about your adult daughter in public.*

What was *wrong* with this man?

"She's struck me as remarkably intelligent and discerning," Rodney countered, in a calm and modulated voice. "She exhibits grace under pressure, and she's tremendously thoughtful. I know she's had some bad luck in the past, but haven't we all?"

Her father's responding smile was tight. "What did you say your name was, again?"

"Dad, *please*," Stacy hissed. "You're embarrassing me."

He looked genuinely taken aback by her comment. "I'm just trying to make sure you're safe," her father said unapologetically. "We don't know this man at all, and . . ."

"I'm not running off to marry him," Stacy said. "And he's not asking for anything."

"Not yet," her father muttered.

Stacy's eyes narrowed. "It's just a date. And a party. Rodney, let's dance."

She wrapped her arm around his waist, leading him to the already crowded floor. A couple dressed in stunning costumes that would've fit in a Baz Luhrmann production danced to the Rolling Stones' *Paint It Black*, while a man in a full football uniform sidled up to what looked like a woman dressed as a sexy . . . bumblebee? What in the world would possess someone to dress as *that*?

"I'm sorry," Stacy said, as she wrapped her arms around him again. "That was a little worse than I expected."

"Don't be. They're just trying to look out for you," he said, squeezing her.

"Because I was wrong before. Reckless, foolish."

"You made a mistake. You trusted someone you shouldn't have. It happens," Rodney said. "But I'm not like that. They'll figure that out. So will you."

She curved against him, tucking her head under his chin. His heart beat faster.

He cared about this woman.

You have to tell her the truth.

"Stacy . . ."

"I will say this, though," she murmured, tilting her head up so he could hear her. "Nobody stands up to him. Even Christian sucked up to him most of the time . . . I'm not sure if I was the main aim, or if he was trying to con my dad. You might've impressed Dad, once he cools down."

"I didn't talk to him to impress him," Rodney said, feeling appalled. "I just didn't like him talking to *you* like that." He paused. "Of course, you can defend yourself. You hardly need me for that. But I understand that family can be difficult to deal with, without doing damage."

"You impressed me." Suddenly, she pressed against him more intimately, kissing his neck. "I don't feel like partying," she said, just below his ear. "Want to get out of here?"

"Yes, but . . ."

This was supposed to be the "proving ground" date. The one where he showed her it was all right for her to trust him. The one where they got to know each other more.

She pulled his head down, pressing her lips against his. Her mouth was hot, sumptuous, and the kiss was hungry. He felt himself respond before his mind knew what was going on, his body going on full alert.

"Come on," she said against his lips, then tugged his hand.

He'd tell her the truth, he thought. Soon. But right now, there were more important things to do.

CHAPTER 10

Stacy couldn't keep her mind focused, but thankfully, she didn't need to. She'd never felt like this, not even with Christian—this white hot need to be with someone, to feel his body against hers, to simply damn thinking altogether and let everything burn.

She took him out a side exit. She took the opportunity to kiss him as the valet that waited there grabbed his car. Her parents' mansion was at the foot of Mount Si, out in the middle of the woods. She didn't feel the January cold, because it felt like she was burning from the inside out.

They took his car—a classy but understated Audi, rather than Esmerelda, she noted with surprise—and she directed him to the town house she lived in, up on the Snoqualmie Ridge. Her stomach jittered nervously, and her pulse pounded like she'd run a marathon.

He looked so damned good in the moonlight, she thought. He smelled wonderful. She rubbed her hand against her lips. He *tasted* wonderful.

"I want you," she whispered, both as a statement of fact and a sort of amazed revelation.

Those sapphire eyes sent her a look that basically melted her panties away. Oh. My. God. She wanted all of him, all at once.

He parked in her driveway, and wordlessly she headed to the front door, trying not to sprint. She felt like she was going to explode if she didn't get her hands on him immediately. She fumbled with the key, her hand shaking.

She felt his hand cover hers, steadying her, easing the key into the lock. *Well, that's Freudian*, she thought, with a hysterical giggle.

"Are you all right?" he asked as they stepped in, closing the door behind them. "I want you, no question. But I don't want you to do anything that you don't feel comfortable with."

"Better than all right." She dropped her keys into the bowl by the door, then turned to look at him. His eyes were dilated and his breathing was ragged.

Hell. Emma and Killian—the Captain Swan ship—had nothing on them.

She took him by the hand, leading him upstairs to the master bedroom. Ordinarily, it was just someplace she changed clothes and slept—she hadn't had any man over since she moved in, shortly after the Christian disaster. Now, the warm amber-painted walls and the rust and ruby comforter seemed unbelievably sensual, the glow from her stained-glass lamp adding to the ambiance.

More than a one-night stand. More than friends.

She wasn't sure what they were starting, and she didn't want to think about it, not now. She knew that just by having him here, she was starting a relationship with him. She was trusting him.

But for tonight, she wanted to just *feel*. Not get into her own head, her own misgivings, the mistakes of her past.

Maybe a little role-playing was in order.

She batted her eyelashes at him, stretching out on the bed. "Now that you have me, Captain, what are you going to do with me?"

He looked surprised for a second, then smiled devilish-ly. "Oh, it's like that, is it?" he asked, his voice warm with humor and laced with passion. "Well, lass . . . I think that I'm going to do things you've never even dreamed of."

"I don't know . . . I've dreamt about it quite a bit," she murmured, slipping off her shoes and reaching for the zipper on the back of her dress.

He stripped off his brocade jacket, leaving him in a black vest and white linen shirt, which he quickly peeled off as well. Her eyes popped for a second—the guy was surprisingly ripped, a nicely muscled chest with just enough definition. *Yum*, her body thought, her heart rac-ing.

"Oh, the look on your face, love," he murmured, smil-ing. "It's enough to make a man feel ten feet tall."

"Are you planning on ravishing me, Captain?" she purred. She'd unzipped the dress—thank God Kyla had made that relatively easy, not a million period-authentic buttons—and held the top of the bodice against herself provocatively, plumping her breasts up over her crossed arms.

His cobalt blue eyes were alight as he took her in. "I'm planning on torturing you," he said. "Both of us, perhaps."

He was still grinning as he strode over to her, crushing their lips together. Her hands smoothed up the broad expanse of his chest as his tongue tangled with hers, his lips massaging hers with passionate abandon. She whimpered with need, pressing her chest against his. The problem was that she had too many clothes on, she thought.

She nudged him away.

"Are you all right . . ." he started to ask, then went silent as she shifted, standing for a second as she stepped out of the red dress, leaving only her lacy white strapless bra and high-cut panties, as well as white stockings and a white garter belt. He made an unintelligible sound.

She leaned back on the bed. "Let's see what you've got," she challenged, feeling deliciously wanton, unbelievably free.

His look was one of almost reverence. Instead of leaping on her as she'd expected, he stretched out beside her. "You're better than I imagined," he breathed. "God, you're stunning."

She started to reach for him, but to her shock, he stopped her. "Remember? Torture. Don't make me tie you up."

She'd never been into that, either . . . but hell, tonight, with this man, she was into anything. "Maybe later."

She saw the second of shock, but then his quick, hungry smile . . . just before his head leaned down, taking her nipple into his mouth, sucking her through the lace. She felt the contrast of textures, the wet heat of his tongue, the smoothness of the silk versus the slight abrasion of the material. He cupped her other breast with his palm, squeezing gently, with a gradually escalating roughness that seemed to take into account what her body craved. She felt her hips lifting off the bed, her thighs rubbing together restlessly. "Rodney . . ." she gasped, aching.

He didn't stop. He tugged down the cup, and the wet heat of his mouth as he took her nipple deeper between his lips was like a shot of molten heat, driving her until she was arching her back to fit herself more deeply into his sensual kiss. She made a soft sound of protest as his hand moved away from her breast, only to quiet immediately as she felt his palm stroke down the plane of her stomach, resting on the soft mound over her clit, over her panties. She took a ragged breath as his teeth softly grazed her nipple.

He shifted from one breast to the other as his fingers delved beneath the waistband of her panties, parting her curls, finding her narrow opening. He flexed his fingers, spreading her open, stroking her. She felt the wave of wetness in response and started moving, her hands reaching for his shoulders, her fingers moving to weave themselves into his hair.

"Slow down, sweetheart . . ." he said, shifting her, tugging her torso up from the bed for long enough to remove the impediment of her bra. His gaze burned her, and he rubbed his goatee lightly against her chest, whispering kisses across her collarbone, her shoulders, the undersides of her breasts. "Torture, for both of us. I swore I'd take my time, but you're a temptation, and you're breaking my good intentions."

The man had more patience than she did, that was for damned sure. She felt his every heated breath as he pressed kisses down her chest, moving lower. He started to tug her panties down, then realized they would get caught up on the garter belt. He paused for a second, frowning.

"Take your time tomorrow," she said, her head lolling on the pillows. "Damn it, Rodney, please . . . please . . ."

"I'll bloody well buy you new ones," he muttered as he simply tore her panties off, leaving the garter belt on. He tossed the ruined undies to one side, gripping her hips, keeping her still as his head went down . . .

She couldn't help twisting as that hot, seeking tongue of his found her swollen clit and started circling it, the flat of his tongue pressing hard and stroking firmly. Her breathing was harsh and broken, her hands making fists in her sheets as her head moved from one side to the other. She could feel it . . . that delicious pressure, building.

"Please," she whispered mindlessly, her body tensing beneath his ministrations. "God, please . . . oh! Yes . . ."

He started working faster, his tongue dancing, flicking, circling, delving against her sex. Then he reached down, pressing two fingers high inside her.

She came in an explosion, shouting as pleasure overwhelmed her. She was breathing hard, feeling floaty and almost numb, as she heard him rip a condom package open. His hands were the ones shaking now, she noticed, as he stripped off the rest of his clothes and rolled the condom onto himself. His cock jutted out impressively, she noticed, and she felt her body start to hunger for the feel of him against her.

When he turned back to her, she smiled, holding out her arms. "Now," she said simply. "I want to feel you inside me."

He let out an incoherent moan and fitted himself over her, the heat of his body melting against hers. His chest hair rubbed against her sensitive, pebble-hard nipples as he kissed her deeply. She sighed and reached down, feeling the heavy hardness of him, guiding him to where she was already wet and dying for him.

He glided in, stretching her, filling her to the point of bursting, but it felt wonderful. It felt better than anything she could ever remember feeling. She lifted her legs, cradling him, wrapping them around his waist, encouraging him to go deeper, deeper . . .

He groaned, pressing his face against her neck. "You are so lovely," he said, his British accent making the words even sexier, the deep, rasping timbre caressing her just as much as his body. He withdrew, then pressed deeper. She lifted her hips to meet his.

Within moments, they were moving, straining together in a furious rhythm. She clawed at his back. He circled his hips ever so slightly, the base of his shaft colliding with her clit as he rammed into her willing warmth. Soon, they were both breathless, both mindless to everything but pleasure.

The pressure was building again, amazingly—and it felt like it would be even stronger, if possible. She struggled, her whole body clenching around him. "I'm . . . I'm going to . . ."

He groaned and grabbed her hips, spearing into her, striking her in that elusive spot that he seemed to find unerringly. She screamed, tugging at his hair, and she felt him shudder, heard him shout his own completion as he came inside her, her own convulsions gripping him tightly.

When it was over, he collapsed to her side, twisting her against him. They lay that way for a long moment, him still buried inside her, their sweat-slicked bodies so close they were practically one as they both let out gulping, gasping breaths.

"Bloody hell, woman," he finally said. "You are a goddess."

She stretched, smiling. "And you, sir, are a pirate."

He smiled. "Give me a few minutes, and maybe we can go again?"

"As soon as I can feel my limbs," she promised, before twining her fingers into his dark hair and dragging him down for another languid kiss.

CHAPTER 11

Rodney woke the next morning to find himself in a strange bed—a comfortable bed. He was spooned up against a woman's soft, supple form.

Stacy.

He sighed as he pressed against her, his body starting to stir to life—which was surprising in and of itself. He was hardly an old man, but it had been some time since he'd had a session of sexual exuberance like the previous night. They'd gotten perhaps two or three hours of sleep, tops, and he'd come on three separate occasions. He'd lost count of how many orgasms Stacy appeared to have had, he thought with a small amount of sleepy satisfaction, holding her tighter.

You have to talk to her, he reminded himself, sobering.

He nuzzled the back of her neck. "Happy New Year," he whispered. *I'm falling in love with you*, he thought as he pressed a kiss on her shoulder, on her neck, where her jawbone met the back of her ear. "You awake?"

"Mmm. It's too early," she murmured, wiggling her backside against him and testing his resolve. "And I'm tired. You wore me out, Captain."

Pirate captain and the saucy wench, he thought with a grin. Oh, yeah. That had been a good one. They'd have to recreate that role-play again soon.

Talk first. Play later.

He propped himself up on one arm, staring at her profile, at the way her wavy hair spilled out across the pillow. He stroked her skin, tracing sloping curves of her body, until she turned to him, hazel eyes glowing, pressing a kiss against his chest.

"Well, since we're both awake . . ." She started to stroke down his stomach.

He held her hand still. "You wore me out, too, lass," he joked. "And I told you: we're not a one-night stand."

She smiled at him, sending him a sexy look from under long lashes. "After a night like that, I don't know how many I'd survive."

"I'm being serious, Stacy," he said gently. "I want a relationship with you, not just a fling."

Her eyes widened. "I know."

He took a deep breath. "So I want to talk with you. Hash some things out."

Tell you who I really am.

"Well, that doesn't quite sound romantic," she said, her full lips pursing.

Before he could speak, his stomach let out a loud, embarrassing howl. He felt his cheeks heat. *Please, God, don't let me be blushing on top of this, as well.*

She laughed, and he grinned back at her. "That's not romantic, either," he admitted.

"Tell you what. Why don't we get cleaned up, and grab some breakfast? Then we can 'hash out' whatever you like."

"That's probably the best plan."

"There's a guest bath downstairs. I'll take a quick shower here, and get cleaned up. I probably look like a raccoon," she said, rubbing at her face. "I never took off my makeup last night. And I need to brush up and stuff."

"Sure you don't want company in that shower?" he asked, as she got up and he saw the sweet curve of her ass, the way her waist nipped in.

"If you join me, we're never going to eat," she replied with a laugh.

Feeling like a freak, he went out to his car in his pirate trousers, grabbing his gym bag. He quickly showered, feeling better. Steeling himself for the conversation. Not that it was that bad: it wasn't like he was hiding a criminal past or had some kind of communicable disease, for God's sake. But he hadn't shared his real identity with women for a reason. He wondered if it would change how Stacy would treat him. Being royalty, such as it was in this day and age, was something that tended to make people look at him like some kind of freak. She'd liked him as a simple coder. Would it be that different, knowing that he was considerably richer than she'd been led to believe?

Which, of course, led to the real problem: he'd been keeping a secret from her.

She'll understand, he reassured himself.

But when he went out into the living room, she was waiting for him, not with a generous smile, but with a frown. Her cell phone was in her hand, and her expression was one of accusation.

"I just got off the phone with my parents," she said, quietly.

"Oh?" He wondered if they'd disapproved of him. At least that was one good thing about being a rich duke: he certainly wouldn't be a gold digger. And he'd stake his family against any of the so-called "acceptable" suitors' families.

She crossed her arms.

"I don't know how, but they managed to do a background check on you."

He blinked, stunned, and a little ball of ice formed in the pit of his stomach. It was good that she knew . . . but from the look of her, she wasn't happy about discovering it. Was it the way she found out? Or the information itself?

"You're not Rodney Charles," she said, her voice jagged with hurt. "You've been lying to me."

"Not exactly," he admitted. "Didn't the background check . . ."

Before he could finish his sentence, she reached behind her, grabbing a knickknack of some sort—a small crystal globe—and hurling it at his head.

"Hey!" he yelped, dodging.

"How . . . could I be . . . this... this..." she said, grabbing more decorative ammo and hurling it at him. "Twice! I was this foolish TWICE!"

"Would you calm down?" he shouted, then realized his mistake almost immediately as her eyes lit for battle. Why would being a duke be this upsetting for her?"

She grabbed a broom, holding it up like a lance. "Get the *fuck* out of my house before I call the cops."

"Stacy, will you *listen* to me?" he said. "I lied to you about who I was, but I had a really good reason."

"Oh, really?" She poked him with the broom, maneuvering him toward the door. "That's what they *all* say. God, can't you do better than that? You know what, *never mind*! I don't want to hear another word!"

"I'm not a con artist, for God's sake," he protested.

"Oh, really? Than who are you, really?"

He let out an irritated *oof* as she poked him hard in the midsection, bumping him against the closed front door. "Didn't the background check tell you who I really am? I'm rich, for God's sake. I don't need your money! And I'm not trying to trick you!"

"You think Christian didn't try that little angle, too? 'I come from a rich family, I got cut off because blah blah blah,' or whatever," she mocked. "They found out that you'd been lying. That's all I need to know."

He grimaced. "But I lied for a valid reason," he pressed, frustrated. "I was trying to become a different person. If your parents got an entire brief on me, they'd have to realize that I . . ."

"That what? You're actually going to try to concoct why you had a good reason to *lie*?" she shouted.

So she didn't know he was a duke, didn't know that he was trying to separate himself from his family's name, wealth, and baggage. And if he told her right now, she'd never believe him. Hell, he wouldn't believe himself, in her position. It would sound like another excuse, and a far-fetched one at that. "Let me prove it. I can prove who I really am, and explain . . ."

"Just. Get. OUT!" She smacked him with the broom.

He opened the door, then grabbed the business end of the broom before she could attack him again. "We're not through here," he said. "If you don't want anything to do with me after you find out who I really am, I'll respect it. But for Christ's sake, you've got to at least give me—*us*—a chance!"

She shoved him out the door, slamming it behind him.

"I'm not giving up on us!" he shouted at her, not caring if he made a scene.

She needed evidence? He'd provide it. The only trick was making sure she'd actually *listen*.

But he wasn't giving up on her, or them, without a fight.

CHAPTER 12

Hours later, Stacy sat in her parents' living room, feeling numb. They'd descended on her house when she was sobbing over Rodney, and insisted that she "come home" so they could take care of her, her mother packing a bag while her father guided her to his car. She hadn't had the energy to resist their well-meaning pressure, so she'd given in, and now she was bundled up on a couch, feeling numb. She'd burned her tongue on the coffee they'd poured for her when she'd arrived, and barely noticed.

Her parents hovered around her, talking, pacing, ranting. She watched them blankly, as if she'd wandered into a lecture in a class she wasn't taking. It was an out-of-body experience.

It couldn't have happened again. I couldn't have made this colossal a mistake twice in my life.

Could I?

God, what is wrong with me?

It was too painful to think about, so her mind had basically shut off, cringing away from any thought of . . . *him*. The pleasure of the previous night. The pain of this morning.

"At least we caught this one in time," her mother said, patting her on the arm. She'd been plying Stacy with iced tea, coffee, some kind of beverage, all morning, it seemed like.

"If he's not Rodney Charles, who exactly is he?" Stacy heard herself ask, and frowned. With her brain trying desperately to protect her, it seemed that one was coming from her heart. Somehow, she held out hope that he had some kind of explanation.

Please don't tell me I fell for a bastard twice.

"The investigator didn't know yet. But does it matter?" her father said, pacing. He'd upgraded from iced tea to gin and tonic by noon and he was still livid. "The guy is using an alias. What normal, law-abiding citizen uses an alias? What normal person doesn't use his real name?"

She could see their point. She hunched lower in the seat. "How did the investigator even find that out?" Stacy asked. "You just found out about Rodney last night. It was at midnight on New Year's Eve. Who works at that hour?"

Her mother looked pained. Her father spun. "We've got a private detective on retainer," he said. "And considering the amount we pay him, he's damned well going to do some digging at one in the morning if I call him. And don't give me that look. It's getting to the point where I want to

105

CATHY YARDLEY

run fingerprints on every man who looks at you at this point. It's like you're a magnet for losers and con artists."

Stacy cringed. Her mother tutted at her husband, then gave Stacy's shoulders a squeeze. "We've just been so worried," she said. "Yes, it may seem crazily overprotective—but after Christian, we're just lucky he wasn't someone who was interested in ransom."

"Christian was a thief," Stacy said.

"It's not a huge leap in criminal terms," her father countered. "Damn it! We vet people for a reason. Is there something wrong with decent, well-bred young men we know, that you've got to go running out and looking for liars and degenerates?"

Silence fell like an ax blade. Stacy had thought nothing could feel worse than finding out that Rodney was a liar about his identity. Apparently, this was worse.

Her parents made it clear that they couldn't trust her. She couldn't trust herself. Which made her a loser herself, didn't it?

The intercom buzzed. "Mr. Fielder? There is a . . . Rodney Charles, here to see Stacy."

Stacy jolted. "He's here?"

"The balls on this guy," her father said. "Kick him out. No, wait—*I'll* kick him out."

"No, Dad," Stacy followed in his wake, her mother trailing behind, making nervous noises. "I'll take care of it."

"Stacy!" she heard Rodney shouting from the foyer. The security guard at the door was with the housekeeper, Mrs. Lance. "Stacy! Damn it, the least you can do is hear me out!"

Her father walked over to Rodney. "You've got about a second before I beat your ass into the floor."

Rodney sighed. "Given your position, I can understand. I lied about my name, and I know your daughter has been hurt before. But I tried to tell her this morning: it has nothing at all to do with her. I can prove this."

"We don't want to hear anything you have to say," her mother said.

"I'd like the chance to mount my own defense," he said. "You have to at least give me that chance!"

"Why should I?" her father thundered.

"Because I'm falling in love with your daughter," Rodney said, his accent so sharp it could cut glass. "Something I do not say lightly and something I find galling to need to relay through intermediaries. She is a grown woman. At least give her the dignity of making her own mind up about me."

"Her judgment," her father said, with derision, "is hardly a reliable factor here!"

And there it was, Stacy realized. Why she'd run off with Christian, perhaps. Why she'd always been attracted to the bad boys. She had acted out, a knee-jerk response to her parents' well-meaning but heavy-handed control.

She was twenty-six years old. She needed to do more than just rebel like some emo teenager. She needed to take the reins of her own damned life.

"I want to hear what he has to say," she said.

Her father turned. "Are you kidding me?"

Her mother interrupted. "Honey, you're distraught."

"No. He's right about one thing," Stacy said. "He shouldn't have lied to me, but I have the right to make the decision based on what I hear, and what he has to say."

"I'm not living through that again," her father said. "If you want to play Russian roulette with your relation-ships, fine. But you're not going to have access to your trust fund. You're not going to ruin your financial future and threaten your family's well-being because you're not thinking straight."

He was waiting for her to roll over. She sighed.

"I'll get a job. A *permanent* job, whether that's at MPG if they want me, or somewhere else," she said. "I'll move out of the town house. And Mom, Dad . . . I love you, but I'm twenty-six years old. Have I made mistakes? Yes. And I will make more. But please. You've got to accept my choices, and let me grow up."

She walked out, Rodney following her. She took a deep breath. "Can you give me a lift to the bookstore?" she asked simply. She knew if she stayed there, her parents would want to interrupt, either to correct her or to grill him. She wanted this to stay between them. And if it all went badly, she knew that her best friends would care for her in a way her parents wouldn't, or possibly couldn't: without judgment, without treating her like a helpless child.

She needed to handle this shit, as Hailey would say, on her own. He nodded, opening the door to his car.

"Thank you," he said.

"Don't thank me yet," she answered. "I'm giving you the chance to explain yourself. That doesn't mean that I'm going to get back with you, or that we're going to be anything after this discussion. Do I make myself clear?"

"Crystal," he replied. He took a deep breath. "Unfortunately, my story is a little . . . unbelievable."

"Of course it is."

"I'm a duke." The words spilled out of his mouth. "And yes, it sounds bloody ridiculous. Especially in light of what your parents are accusing, and what you've gone through in the past. But I am."

"And you drive a BMW and live in an apartment with Fezza."

"Next door to Fezza, but yes."

"Well, then," she said, shaking her head. "I'm certainly glad you cleared the air."

He sighed. "You don't believe me. I knew you wouldn't."

"Of course I don't believe you!" she exploded. "Because it's ridiculous!"

He pulled over, and looked at her. "I know it sounds insane. But I was . . . bored. Stifled. My family's quite wealthy. I'm a titled heir, but all I wanted to do was make video games," he said, sounding rather impassioned. God help her, he sounded like he was telling the truth.

But didn't they all?

"I changed my name because I couldn't very well go around introducing myself as Roderick Andrew Murray Fitzclarence, the twelfth Duke of St. Charles," he said. "I left England because I wanted to leave that behind. I wanted to get by on my own merits. Whatever else can be said about the United States, you believe in a man making it on his own, not because of how he was born. And when I became a game designer, it was because I could code, not because of a title and who I went to bloody school with!"

She stared at him. "Why didn't you tell me before now?"

"Do you know how many women have tried to 'land' me . . . the titled heir to a fortune? Do you know how many women tried to *sue* me, on trumped-up charges of paternity? Who sold details of my life to tabloids?" He looked at her sadly. "I wanted you to care about me for me. As a guy who wears T-shirts and jeans and occasionally needs to be bailed out of the parking lot because Fezza's car needs to be towed. I wanted you to see me as *normal*."

"I wouldn't say you're normal," she said with a watery laugh. "But that doesn't mean I didn't like you."

He sighed. Then he pulled out an iPad. "Here. Look. I've queued it up."

"What am I looking at?" she said.

"Who I really am." He winced, and his expression was one of embarrassment. "Or at least, who I was. Some of these articles are old."

She stared. These were online versions of British tabloids. There were grainy pictures that were obviously of him. Partying in Ibiza, having scandalous "affairs" with various women, holding up a hand against obviously invasive paparazzi. A picture of him in mourning, with his mother, commenting on the death of his father, the previous duke.

Duke of St. Charles, Earl of Loamshire. Most eligible bach-elor.

She stared at him.

"You're a duke? Really?"

He nodded. "I didn't want you to know. Didn't want anybody to know," he said. "But then I fell for you, and I knew you *had* to know. But before I could tell you, your parents did a shit job exposing only the fact that I lied . . . and not what I lied about."

"I can't believe this."

"I didn't lie to hurt you," he said. "I was wrong, and the timing was bad . . . but please, believe me. I never wanted to hurt you."

She nodded. Her chest felt warm, and she realized that tears were starting to trickle down her cheeks. He wiped them away with his thumbs.

"Forgive me?" he said. "I swear, if you trust me . . . I'll do everything I possibly can to make it up to you."

She went quiet, turning inside. Not thinking of what her parents wanted, or what she'd experienced with Christ-ian. Listening to her gut.

The one that said to trust him, even when she didn't know his real name.

"I do trust you," she said quietly. "I always did, some-how. I just didn't trust myself."

He leaned over, kissing her, and she kissed him back enthusiastically.

"But if you screw up like this again, and lie to me," she said, between kisses, "I am frickin' murdering you with that broom."

"If I lie to you again," he said, laughing and kissing her harder, "I'll stand there and let you."

EPILOGUE

One month later . . .

"I can't believe this," Stacy breathed, as Rodney helped her off the private jet.

"What? You've been to England before."

She gave him a gentle shove. "I've never been in a private jet before, and certainly haven't landed on the private airstrip of a big English mansion."

"Seat of the family's estates," he admitted, looking a tiny bit sheepish. She noticed that he'd certainly dressed the part. Gone were the ironic T-shirt and jeans and sneakers she was used to. He was wearing a dark charcoal suit with a snowy white shirt and a deep blue tie that matched his eyes. He looked scrumptious, every inch the English lord-of-the-manor. Although in this case, she supposed duke-of-the-manor was more appropriate.

"So . . . all this is yours?"

"Yes, quite." He put his hands in his pockets, suddenly looking boyish. "Not put off, are you?"

He sounded like he was joking, but there was a serious look in his eyes—a studying. As if to see if a dollar sign radar was going to suddenly light up in her eyes. She shook her head.

"It's going to be pretty tough to take," she drawled, then grinned. "I would've fallen in love with you, even if you were just a coder, driving Fezza's beater car."

His answering smile was like sunlight on the overcast day. "Nonsense. No woman in her right mind would fall in love with a man who owns that damned junker."

She grinned, and let him escort her to the mansion.

Thanks for reading Stacy and Rodney's story! Next up: One True Pairing. *Hailey Frost is a badass who would do anything to help her sisters — including fake a relationship with celebrity Jake. But what happens when she's finally tempted to fall in love?*

A NOTE FROM CATHY

Thank you so much for reading *Hooked!* I enjoyed exploring the *Once Upon a Time* fandom, and I hope you had fun with it, too.

The Fandom Hearts series is all about finding the things you're passionate about — the things you're *geeky* about — and going all in. I loved writing this series, and I hope you enjoy reading it just as much. The series is complete (I think? For now? Although some of those secondary characters *have* been nudging at me!) and each book can be read as a stand-alone, although they can be enjoyed in chronological series order for the full experience. And there are other series to enjoy if you're looking for more fun, geeky love stories!

If you do enjoy the book, please take a minute to write a review of this on Amazon and Goodreads. Reviews make a huge difference in an author being discovered in book

CATHY YARDLEY

searches
and shared with other readers!

And if you'd like to connect with me, I love hearing from readers! You can stop by www.CathyYardley.com to email me, or visit me on social media. Or join my Facebook readers group, _Can't Yardley Wait,_ to see early reveals, exclusive content, and a lot of shenanigans with a very fun group.

Enjoy!
Cathy

ABOUT THE AUTHOR

Cathy Yardley writes fun, geeky, and diverse characters who believe that underdogs can make good and sometimes being a little wrong is just right.

She likes writing about quirky, crazy adventures, because she's had plenty of her own: she had her own army in the Society of Creative Anachronism; she's spent a New Year's on a 3-day solitary vision quest in the Mojave Desert; she had VIP access to the Viper Room in Los Angeles.

Now, she spends her time writing in the wilds of Eastern Washington, trying to prevent her son from learning the truth of any of said adventures, and riding herd on her two dogs (and one husband.)

Want to make sure you never miss a release? For news about future titles, sneak peeks, and other fun stuff, please sign up for Cathy's newsletter here.

LET'S GET SOCIAL

Hang out in Cathy's Facebook group, Can't Yardley Wait

Talk to Cathy on Twitter

See silly stuff from Cathy's life on Instagram

Never miss a release! Follow on Amazon

Don't miss a sale — follow on BookBub

ALSO BY CATHY YARDLEY

THE PONTO BEACH REUNION SERIES

Love, Comment Subscribe

Gouda Friends

Ex Appeal

THE FANDOM HEART SERIES

Level Up

Hooked

One True Pairing

Game of Hearts

What Happens at Con

Ms. Behave

Playing Doctor

Ship of Fools

SMARTYPANTS ROMANCE

Prose Before Bros

STAND ALONE TITLES

The Surfer Solution

Guilty Pleasures

Jack & Jilted

Baby, It's Cold Outside

Printed in Great Britain
by Amazon

29206773R00069